This is the most beautiful place I've ever seen. You must show me everything.

As familiar as every reef was to her, she never dared let down her guard. Captain Bobby Raffin had drummed the lesson into her over and over – the first rule of the sea. "Never close your eyes to the sea, my girl. And never turn you back on it. It can snap back at you as fast as a cat with a mouse." Yet he always added, "Only remember this too. You're never alone out there. In the roughest sea, in the strongest wind, Someone is watching over you. Our Lord Jesus never forgets us, March." Now, concentrating on her course, March wondered whether the man beside her was questioning her ability, wondered too whether perhaps he would have been happier if his charter captain had really been Mark. She would not take her eyes from the course to look at him, but she could feel that he had not moved from his position at her side. When they had passed the first of the reefs she let her breath out in a small puff that she was sure was not audible over the wind's rush.

"Very nicely done, Captain," Simon Wade said, and he sounded easy and relaxed. If he had been nervous about her navigating he at least kept it out of his voice.

"Thank you," she said crisply. And then she added, "There are more reefs up ahead, of course."

How true that was, she thought.

FLOWER OF THE SEA

Amanda Clark

Serenade/Serenata
BOOKS
of the Zondervan Publishing House
Grand Rapids, Michigan

A Note From The Author

I love to hear from my readers! You may correspond with me by writing:

Amanda Clark
1415 Lake Drive, S.E.
Grand Rapids, MI 49506

FLOWER OF THE SEA
Copyright © 1985 by The Zondervan Corporation
Grand Rapids, Michigan

Serenade/Serenata is an imprint of Zondervan Publishing House,
1415 Lake Drive, S.E., Grand Rapids, Michigan 49506.

ISBN 0-310-46882-5

Edited by Pamela M. Jewell
Designed by Kim Koning

Printed in the United States of America

85 86 87 88 89 90 91 / 10 9 8 7 6 5 4 3 2 1

CHAPTER 1

"SEPARATES," pronounced Melissa with an air of having come to a decision. "Separates are what you are going to need. Come on, March. I see just the sort of thing we're after."

"Really, I don't need anything, Melissa. Honestly, I don't," March protested, following in her cousin's wake, threading her way among racks and counters in the plush Fifth Avenue department store. "I won't be dressing up much—and I'll only be there a few weeks. Why don't we wait till I come back?"

But kind-hearted Melissa was unstoppable. "Nonsense. It will lift your spirits. You need that more than anything, and you need it right now, not later. Later will take care of itself."

If only it would, March thought glumly. But at the moment the future looked as bleak as the present. All she had to cling to was the past, and she would be a fool to do that. The past was gone forever.

"You've already spent far too much on me—I feel I must begin to pay you back, and I will too, as soon as things are settled back home. But I just can't accept any more."

7

"Now this would be a good color for you," Melissa said, ignoring March's protests and picking from the rack a turquoise-blue cotton skirt. "See, they have it in green too. We'll take both. Now let's look for a few tops. And what do you think—espadrilles—to go with them? We can get them in different colors. That should be just right for the island."

"I usually wear jeans and a denim shirt," March said timidly.

"Well, that's not a law, is it? Here, take these into the fitting room," Melissa ordered. "I'll bring you some tops to try. You'll need something new to wear on the plane too. "

In the curtained fitting room March tried on the skirts and then the tops that Melissa kept thrusting in at her. "Here's a color that would be heavenly on you. Try this one, dear. It's just meant to go with your eyes. And here's one in yellow."

March sighed and looked at herself in the glass, then turned and saw three reflections, three March Raffins standing there in the bright new resort-looking clothes. Heart-shaped face, honey-colored hair falling softly around her shoulders, eyes the color of the sea where it shoaled up clear and shallow around the island's hidden coves. The blouse Melissa had just handed her had a peasant neckline with a drawstring, short-puffy sleeves and pale blue embroidery trim. In spite of her dull gray mood, March admired it—it *did* have the effect of lifting her spirits—but only for a moment, because at once she remembered the trip that lay ahead of her, and something inside her went plummeting again. The warm atmosphere of the store seemed suddenly stifling and she longed to be outside even in the chilly drizzle of the New York day.

"They're all heavenly on you," Melissa declared when March emerged with the pile of clothes over her arm. "You'd better let me do the choosing. Then after we're through here I'm going to stop in at the linens department for some things I need."

8

"Melissa, would you mind—I mean—could I meet you in a few minutes?" March said, trying to keep her voice from trembling. "I think I need a bit of fresh air."

Melissa's kind, plump face looked suddenly concerned. "Of course, dear. Go out and take a little walk for yourself. Tell you what—let's have tea at that restaurant across the street. That'll pick us up nicely. Meet you in half an hour."

"All right." March tried to smile as she left her cousin and pushed her way through the crowded store to the street, but the heavy weight was still inside her and her eyes misted over with tears before she reached the sidewalk. She thrust her hands into the pockets of her raincoat and started walking aimlessly up Fifth Avenue, past St. Patrick's Cathedral, past the smart shops, up one side and then across and down the other. The air was chilly and full of a fine cold mist that settled in her hair and turned it into curling tendrils around her forehead. She passed the restaurant where she was to meet Melissa and paused to look at her watch. A quarter of an hour yet; she walked on.

Suddenly she found herself standing in front of the brightly lighted window of a travel agency. Colorful posters decorated it, all of them beckoning passersby to palm-fringed beaches, exotic shores, flower-filled nights, gourmet dining. March saw a couple coming out of the agency, their hands full of brochures and pictures. They were laughing and looking at each other, excited about a trip they were planning, she supposed. Another couple went in, an older, retired-looking couple, but there was the same inquisitive eagerness about them. March put her hand on her shoulder bag, thinking about the plane tickets that were already resting there. Tickets that would take her to an island as lovely as any in the lighted window. Lovelier, to her at least, because it was home. And when she went there, day after tomorrow, it would be the saddest moment of her life, because she would be going for the last time. In a few weeks she would be back in New York and would never see her island again. Never. That was a word she was certainly getting used to. These past weeks she had had to. She would never see her father again either. Captain Bobby, everyone on the island had always called him. Captain Bobby Raffin with his sun-burned, weather-roughened face, the laugh-crinkles around his eyes, his sandy hair sprinkled with gray. March turned away from the window, blinking back tears, and hurried toward the restaurant.

It had been Melissa who had come to her rescue six months before, when Captain Bobby had first fallen ill.

"You must bring him here, March. Bill says by all means bring him here where he can have the very finest care and Bill can keep an eye on him himself." Her husband, a prominent New York surgeon, had gotten on the phone then and urged her himself. "Don't be ridiculous!" he had shouted in his hearty good-natured way. "It's not a bit of trouble. You'll stay here with us—Melissa will love having you—and we'll meet your plane. We'll have that fellow fit in no time."

They had comforted and sustained March then, too, these faraway cousins whom she saw so seldom. And indeed, no one could have worked harder than Dr. Bill Brauner, calling in specialist after specialist and refusing to give up until the very end. But there were some things, as he told her gently, holding both her hands in his large ones, before which the whole medical fraternity was still powerless.

"I know you did everything you could," March said simply, and managed not to break down until she was alone. But the breaking down was only a personal reaction to the loss of a loved one, to the ending of a

10

vigil—six months of waiting, hoping, praying. Afterward she was able to mourn her loss while still saying, *Thy will be done,* and a deep sustaining comfort swelled in her heart at the sure and certain knowledge that life everlasting awaited Captain Bobby Raffin. It was a conviction that had brought comfort and meaning to his life, and he had passed it on to her. Briefly she thought of the inestimable value of that gift. Then, squaring her shoulders, she turned back to the decisions that awaited her. Bill and Melissa had urged her to come to New York to live, and she knew their view was a practical one. So it had been decided that she would return home to Coral Cay in the Bahamas. She would sell Captain Bobby's boat, the *Flower of the Sea,* along with their little house and its furnishings. Once matters there were concluded she would come back to New York, where a job would be waiting for her as a receptionist and clerical worker for a group of doctors sharing offices near the hospital she had come to know so well these last months. "And you can take some courses in your off hours," Dr. Bill Brauner had said. "Medical technology, medical secretary—whatever appeals to you—so that you'll be able to move ahead to better jobs."

"And you can stay here with us," Melissa had chimed in.

"Oh, Melissa, I couldn't do that."

"Silly, we love having you. But if you really feel you must be off on your own, I'll help find you an apartment. I'm sure you'll even find some girl who'll become a friend—probably in your new job—and you can share an apartment and expenses."

"And you'll get used to going out and meeting people. Goodness, you've been too stuck away back there on your precious island. Well, I know you love it and it's beautiful and all that, but for heaven's sake, March, you needed to move into the world—have men friends. Who knows, you might even meet . . . ''

"All right," March had interrupted hastily, seeing Melissa embarked on a whole new train of thought leading to marrying her off. "All right. I guess that's the best thing for me to do."

"Well, of course it is. Goodness, you can't stay there alone!"

But I never felt alone on the island, March thought wonderingly. *Even when Captain Bobby went off somewhere in the Flower of the Sea—escorting a party of tourists perhaps—even when I was alone in the house I never felt alone. There was always the hotel, where my best friend Pauline and her parents lived—the people who owned the hotel. Don and Marian Sanders and Pauline were always there if I needed them. And Miss Emily in the hotel kitchen with all her bubbling pots and pans and all the tempting smells of island cooking. And the rest of the islanders—I knew them all by name.*

"Then it's settled," Melissa had said in her firm, decisive way. "Now the thing to do is get you ready."

And now, sitting across the small table in the restaurant filled with other weary shoppers, Melissa said much the same thing.

"Now I think you're really ready, dear. Clothes, airplane ticket, luggage. Now don't take my head off, March, but I bought you a new suitcase. They'll deliver it later this afternoon."

"Oh, Melissa," March shook her head in despair.

"And that leaves just tomorrow. You can have your hair done."

"My hair—" March's hand flew to her head and the unruly curls that the misty day had created. "It's all right, Melissa, really. I'll wash it myself and pull it back like I always do."

"Nonsense. It'll do you good to spend a few hours in Rene's. I'll go too, just for the fun of it. We'll make it a day and have lunch out and really pamper ourselves. You know, I've been thinking. If you pack carefully, I think you can do with just one suitcase, and maybe your tote bag. You can leave your warm winter things here. What will the weather be like there, do you think?''

"The weather? Oh, it'll be—" March hesitated and suddenly, almost against her will, the whole feeling and look of the islands washed over her like one of the great waves that curled over the rocky beach near the marina at home. Now, in early April, the spring breezes would be blowing, bending the tall Australian pines and whispering in the huge fig tree that over-hung the little pink house. The oleanders would be in bloom—pink, white, rose – and the hibiscus. All the palm trees would be making a soft papery sound as the breeze rustled them. "It'll be fine for the things we picked out today," she said quietly, looking quickly down at her plate and the untouched croissant Melissa had ordered for her. She sipped at her tea to cover the sudden enexpected emotional surge that had over-taken her, but sharp-eyed Melissa had not been fooled. "I know it's hard for you, dear,' ' she said kindly. "But you will get over it in time. I promise you will. There's a great deal of strength in you, March.''

March nodded without speaking, but to herself she acknowledged the source of that strength, thinking again as she had just after her father's death that it was the all-encompassing love of Jesus Christ that bolstered her and lent resolution to her soul.

If her heart had been a little lighter, March had to admit the experience of an afternoon at Rene's would have been enjoyable. Being pampered, fussed over, complimented—"My dear young lady, I know wom-en who would *kill* for hair like that"—was something completely new to her. In fact, Rene, himself, person-ally supervised her hair.

"What we want here, Wallace, is to frame her face

and taper gradually to the shoulders, just so." March let the combing, cutting, and brushing relax her and was almost startled when it was done. Then she was whisked to another area of the salon. Here Elaine and Rita, two women with dramatic makeup and long perfect nails, began massaging her hands and feet with warm oils. After an hour of trimming, shaping and buffing, March emerged with immaculately groomed nails that blushed with a hint of pale translucent polish. Her hair softly framed her face and fell to just above her shoulders. She stared at her reflection in the mirror, trying to accustom herself to the stranger looking back at her.

"Now *that's* more like it," Melissa said approvingly.

Bill and Melissa were both at Kennedy airport with her the next day to see her off. Melissa kept fussing over her and asking her questions ten times over. Was she quite sure she'd have no trouble with her bag while changing planes in Florida? Had she remembered to pack everything? Would anyone there be expecting her? What sort of state would the house be in after six months? And March kept soothing her and answering that she would be fine, there was no cause for worry.

"At least you have a seat in first class," Melissa said, brushing imaginary lint from the sleeve of March's cream-colored blazer. The blazer matched the skirt she was wearing, and a soft, pastel blouse completed the outfit. "We want you to enjoy this trip, as much as it's possible for you to, anyway."

"Oh Melissa—Bill—that wasn't necessary," March protested, but practical Bill waved her objections away.

"When can we expect you back?" he asked.

March hesitated. "Why it will take me a little time to see about selling the house and the boat. And there

14

are other things to take care of, Dad's things to pack away, and—oh, I just don't know exactly. But no more than a few weeks, I suppose." Why was she being evasive about it? It was all settled. She had agreed. And certainly what Bill and Melissa wanted for her was the wisest, most sensible course. Indeed, she should count herself lucky to have a kind and caring couple like the Brauners to help her. Bill must have juggled a dozen important appointments to come here to the airport today.

He looked down at her, studying her intently. "You know, honey, when difficult things have to be done, sometimes it's best to do them quickly. Get the bad part over with."

"Yes, I know," March agreed. Then she brightened and tried to smile. "I'll write to you when I get there and let you know how things look and how soon I can get back. Okay?"

"Okay," Melissa said, close to tears herself and hugging March. "I know I've been terribly bossy, but I just feel like a mother and a sister too. And I do worry about you."

"You've been wonderful," March assured her. A voice sounded over the loudspeaker and Bill said, "All right, that's your flight. Come along. Your bag's all checked in and here's your boarding pass."

Once on the plane, March felt a sense of relief. She had reached the point where even the kindest concern had become oppressive. She longed to be by herself and to give in, just for a time, to all the feelings that were crowding in on her. Not in weeping and self-pity, but just in thinking quietly about her father and home and the island, all the things she would soon be saying goodbye to forever.

She found herself assigned to a window seat next to a middle-aged business man who gave her a polite nod and then at once produced an attaché case full of charts, graphs, and computer printout sheets that he began to study, and only pushed aside when, shortly after takeoff, the stewardess came to spread white tablecloths on their serving tables. March was unable to summon up much appetite for the array of delectable food brought around but reluctantly agreed to the dinner of filet mignon with salad and baked potato. It seemed an overwhelming amount of food to March, whose appetite had been meager of late, but she struggled valiantly with it. When the tables had been cleared and the businessman beside her had taken up his papers again, she let her head rest back against the seat and turned indifferently to look out the window. The cabin was quieter now, the clatter of dishes muted, and for the first time March became aware of the conversation of a man and woman sitting behind her. Preoccupied as she had been, March had paid no attention to them when she was boarding.

Both voices were low and well modulated. The man's was deep and resonant – a voice that tried to be reasonable, March decided. Yet it seemed to her that there was some impatience in it too. She longed to turn and look at him; she found herself curious about who might own such a voice, but she felt shy about doing so. The woman's held sadness, she thought. Although it was an exquisitely clear, cultivated voice, there was no joy in it. They spoke together in low tones but now and then she could make out snatches of the conversation.

"You'll have plenty of company," she heard the man say. "Ed will be calling you as soon as he knows you're there."

"Ed's very sweet, but you mustn't—I mean, I don't want you telling him to look out for me. Now positively not, darling."

"Oh, all right. But really, Diana, it's much better this way."

"But what about you?" The woman's voice held a pleading note. "Won't I be seeing you soon?"

16

"Yes, of course. I'll be coming over when I can. Only I must tend to business first." He was beginning to sound querulous, March thought.

"And of course you have to consider Penny. She'll be joining you, I suppose."

"It hasn't been decided yet."

A broken-off love affair, March thought. He's trying to be kind but final about it—she's clinging to a last hope. She longed to see what they looked like. When the man in the seat next to her rose, stretched, and walked down the aisle to speak to a stewardess, March too got up and stretched as though it were a contagious idea. Then, casually, she managed a stealthy half-turn so that she could look at the two people behind her.

The couple matched their voices, she thought at once. The man, who had the aisle seat, must have been well over six feet tall. His long legs were stretched casually into the aisle as if there was no point in even attempting to cramp them into the inadequate space in front of him. His hair was dark and curly and he had brown eyes slightly uptilted at the corners. The dark, sharply arching eyebrows over them gave him a restless, intense look. March saw how they moved impatiently from his companion to the newspaper he held on his lap. He was dressed in a tweed sports jacket, exquisitely tailored to fit his broad shoulders, and dark slacks. His off-white shirt was open at the neck. The woman beside him was also dark haired, but her hair was smooth and caught back in a classic knot. Her pearl earrings and pearl necklace perfectly complimented the simple, but unmistakably expensive, green silk dress she wore. Her face had high cheekbones and perfect features. She had a languid, elegant look, but there was, as March had suspected, sadness in her pale oval face just as in her voice. The two of them were so striking that for a moment March could not help staring. Then

17

suddenly the man looked up and confronted her gaze. He frowned, and his dark eyes returned her look with an aloofness that seemed to be part annoyance. He seemed irritated, and March, realizing how rude her staring must look, sat down at once, her cheeks burning. Yet in spite of her embarrassment, she found herself almost at once doing something she had done ever since she was a child—spinning an imaginary story in her mind about these unknown people, this cool and elegant couple. They were lovers, and they were breaking up. The affair was over – for him at least. One could sense the restlessness in him. The woman was trying to hang on. She did not want him to provide a substitute—the unknown Ed, whoever he might be. He longed to be rid of her once and for all, but she clung to hope. *Won't I be seeing you soon?* And there was another unknown in the picture. The Penny the woman referred to. A wife in the background, perhaps. *She'll be joining you, I suppose.* So he is deceiving two women, March thought. Remembering the cold, censuring look he had turned on her she felt with a kind of intuitive certainty that he was heartless where women were concerned. She wondered what would happen at the airport in Florida. Would they part at once or leave together?

She heard the woman's voice and it echoed her own thoughts.

"After we land, will you come with me for a little while?"

His voice had the sound of impatience strained to the breaking point. "Darling, I have things to do. I mustn't waste time. You'll be perfectly all right. Go out shopping. Buy yourself a new outfit." March could tell it was all he could do to keep anger out of his voice. And he wasn't giving an inch. She suspected he had an unbending will once his mind was made up.

She saw them embrace later after the plane had

18

landed and the luggage had been claimed. The woman
clung to him for a moment and then, sure enough, he
pulled away and bundled her brusquely into a taxi.
March lost track of him then as she made her way to
the counter to get a seat for her flight in the eight-
passenger Cessna that would take her to Coral Cay.

The ticket agent took her new suitcase and tote bag
and weighed them. "And your own weight, Miss?"

"One hundred fifteen pounds," March said, although she wondered if she had not lost a few pounds
these past six months. He handed her a boarding pass
and said, "There'll be just a short wait, Miss."

As she turned away from the counter she saw the
tall stranger from the New York flight approaching,
putting down his bag and reaching in his pocket for a
ticket. Once more March stared, this time with her
lips parted in astonishment. He was going to Coral
Cay! But what on earth was someone like that
planning to do on such a small insignificant island?
Could he be a fishing enthusiast? Possibly. Some of
the best fishing in the Bahamas was off Coral Cay. Or
maybe he was a swimmer—he had a long lean
swimmer's build, she thought. But there was swimming everywhere. Again, why pick Coral Cay! And
where would he be staying? He might be renting one
of the modest cottages on the island, but somehow
that idea did not seem to suit him either. As for the inn
at Coral Cay—March thought briefly of its shady
veranda, its worn carpets, its well-used furnishings,
comfortably but undisguisedly old. She could not
picture him in *that* setting either. A few tourists,
familiar faces, returned year after year to the inn, but
none of them with this look of wealth and status, of
faintly supercilious worldliness.

"Your weight, sir?" the agent inquired.

"One hundred eighty pounds," the man answered
crisply, and March found herself staring again. It was
certainly a well-distributed one hundred eighty

pounds, she thought. Not an ounce of fat on the long lean torso, the athlete's legs, the square muscular shoulders. His hands, she saw as he reached out for his boarding pass, were long-fingered and brown, the nails square-cut as though for efficiency.

As they boarded the small plane moments later he was once more behind her. As she half turned, she had a fleeting glimpse of him stooping slightly to accommodate his tall frame. She looked away quickly, but she was still aware of his presence as a tangible thing—a kind of invisible electrical energy that seemed to communicate itself to her.

"May I help you with that?" he said as she struggled to shove her tote bag under the seat.

"Thank you," she answered in a small voice, watching him stow it securely with one quick thrust.

"May I?" he asked again, and nodded toward the seat beside her.

"Oh yes. Of course," she answered, feeling again the odd and faintly disturbing communication of energy from him that she had been aware of before. Energy, and perhaps something more. But for the moment she was reluctant to try and analyze her own reaction to him.

Once they were airborne, she felt all earlier concerns slipping away from her. Her surroundings, the small plane with its passengers whom she had not even bothered to notice, the anxieties that had been plaguing her, even the man beside her, all fell away and dropped out of her consciousness. She became aware of only the sky and the sea. Below her the deep ocean water was vivid sapphire, but after a time, as the islands themselves came into distant view and the Great Bahama Bank rose up to make the water shallower, it turned to turquoise or here and there a pale azure blue. *Home*, March thought, and the word drummed in her head like the pounding of rain in one of the island's tropical storms. *Home, home, home.*

And soon she would be leaving it, turning her back on it forever, trading it for a gray city of concrete and cold, for a stiff white uniform and a nine-to-five existence. Her two hands gripped each other in her lap until the knuckles turned white. She closed her eyes tight.

"It's quite safe," the man beside her said suddenly in a calm voice, and March's eyes flew open. "These small planes are a bit scary after the big jets, but there's really very little danger."

"Oh, I wasn't—"

"Just put your mind on something else until we land. Best not to think about it."

He was surely trying to be kind, March thought. And how could she explain that she had made this short trip to and from Florida many times? That the last thing in the world she was feeling was fear, but something else entirely? All at once emotions that she had been holding back ever since her father's death seemed to come crowding in on her, pressing upon her so heavily that suddenly there was no holding them back. The chain of islands and the blue water lay flung out beneath the little plane and she tried hard to concentrate on the islands, to look away from the man so that he would not see the tears gathering in her eyes. But this arrival on Coral Cay would be different from all previous ones. Other times, when she and her father had gone to Florida on business or for boating supplies, he had been returning with her. And even when, now and then, she had gone by herself, he had always been there at the little airstrip to meet her. "Ahoy there, Matey!" he had always sung out, waving to her.

It was no use. Tears brimmed over, spilling down her cheeks, and an audible sob caught in her throat. She could feel the man's eyes on her, and then his voice, sounding dryer now and holding a sardonic note, said, "Well. This seems to be my day for

21

emotional women. Here." And he thrust a linen handkerchief into her hand. Through her tears she saw the fuzzy outlines of a monogram, SW, in one corner.

She tried to thank him, but the words got stuck somewhere. She wiped her eyes and blew her nose, realizing that she must be starting to look frightful. The handkerchief had a clean masculine scent—not cologne, she thought, but more the man himself—a tweed-and-outdoors smell. She managed to stammer at last, "It's very kind. . .thank you. I'm so sorry. . ."

Perhaps he was trying to be kind, March thought, but all the same she found resentment growing in her at his faintly patronizing tone. Emotional women— that did not describe her at all, she thought indignantly. And who was he to intrude on her grief with his pat remedies? What she had taken for kindness began to look suspiciously like smugness and superiority. Having disposed of one woman back in Florida he was undoubtedly feeling quite sure of himself. I can manage this one too, she could almost hear him telling himself.

She pulled herself together and managed to say with some dignity, "If you let me know where you're staying on Coral Cay I'll return your handkerchief."

He gave her a look of amusement that infuriated her for a moment. Dark eyebrows arched upward and the odd, dark eyes with their upturned corners studied her. "Please keep it," he said. "I believe I can spare it."

Her glance took in his expensive-looking attaché case, the richly polished leather of his loafers, the tweed jacket that she was sure was imported, and she felt her cheeks coloring with embarrassment. She looked away from him again, and then he said, still with the amusement in his voice, "You must have been studying up for your vacation. You pronounced that correctly."

"What?" she frowned at him.

"You said Coral *Key*. Not Coral *Kay*. Most tourists mispronounce it."

"Now it was her turn to feel amusement. "Really?"

"Yes. Cay is the Spanish word for island. Of course, Coral Cay is not really an island—not in the strictest sense of the word, although most people refer to it that way. It's a spit of land extending from Coral Harbor, and curved in such a way that it forms a natural harbor—a very fine one, actually."

Again the faintly supercilious tone annoyed her. So he thought she was a little secretary spending her savings on a two-weeks vacation. Well, let him think what he liked. Even though Coral Cay was a small place she had no doubt she would be able to avoid him for whatever time he was there. Once again she turned to look out the window, and this time she kept her face firmly away from him, watching until she could see the familiar shape of Coral Cay, looking, from this altitude, completely wooded and green, with only a narrow strip of beach and a few roofs visible where the inn and marina were. And then the clearing of the small airfield appeared surprisingly in the midst of green pines and she felt the Cessna touch down smoothly.

"March! That was simply awful—you staying away six months! Don't you ever dare do it again!" Pauline Sanders, her oldest and closest friend was the first person she saw after alighting from the plane. Pauline, rosy and windblown and standing beside her battered Volkswagen, waved furiously and then ran to meet her. "Oh, you look wonderful. A little pale, but wonderful. Come on. We'll see about your luggage and then get right to the inn. You'd probably love a bath. Oh March, it's been simply awful—I hadn't anybody to *talk* to with you away!"

March laughed and hugged her back, knowing that

cheerful Pauline could no more help talking than she could help breathing.

"I'm glad I was missed," she said, not wanting to spoil their reunion by telling Paulie that she was not back for good but only for a short stay and that then she would be gone forever.

Paulie held her at arms' length for a moment and said, "March, I know you don't want to talk about it, but I have to say it just once. We all miss Captain Bobby—just terribly. Maybe not as much as you do—but we all loved him so—"

"You're wrong, Paulie," March answered quietly. "I do want to talk about it. And talk and talk and talk. I want to remember everything about him and all the good times. I don't want to forget any of it. And don't you dare avoid the subject, any of you."

As they retrieved her suitcase and wedged it into the Volkswagen, March's eyes skimmed around the tiny airport, but there was no sign of the man who had sat beside her. The island's venerable taxi had been there waiting for any stray tourists. No doubt he had taken that to wherever he was going.

They started down the narrow, pine-bordered road toward the hotel and marina with Paulie still chattering happily. "March, you look absolutely super. Your hair—and that outfit! I think you're thinner, though—oh, I absolutely am going to lose five pounds. This time I really mean it. You just look—I don't know—elegant."

March smiled inwardly, thinking to herself how plain she had felt on the trip from New York when she compared herself with the cool and languid beauty of the woman in the seat behind her. Ah well, all judgments were relative, she supposed. Her old friend's chatter was so welcome to March and all the sights and sounds and sea-smells of the island so blissfully familiar that for a moment all her anxieties fell away from her. She was home, and never mind for how long. Never mind what lay ahead. She was home.

24

"Paulie, will you take me to my house first?" she asked suddenly. "To the foot of the path, I mean? I want to change and rest for a few minutes before I come to the hotel."

"Oh, but March, they're all waiting for you—Mom and Dad and Miss Emily—everybody—"

"I know, and I'll come right away. Just give me a half hour to change and unpack and I'll be there."

"All right, sweetie. I know you. You want a few minutes by yourself. Only I'll come up the path with you to help with your suitcase." She paused. "Later on why don't we go up to our special place—just you and me, March?"

"Oh Paulie, yes. How dear of you to think of it." Their special place was a clearing in the woods that looked out over the sea, and through the years many problems had been worked out, many fears erased, as the two girls prayed together there.

March looked gratefully at the girl beside her. Paulie surely did know her. The two of them had been best friends since before they could walk. And when her own mother had died, two-year-old March had become as much a part of the inn and the Sanders household as Paulie. They had gone to the island's one-room schoolhouse together, sung in the church choir together—although Paulie always insisted she sounded like a crow beside March—arranged each other's hair, experimented with violent shades of nail polish together.

Paulie left her after helping to lug her suitcase up the narrow wooded path to the house, a small pink cottage nestled among the tall pines through which a glimpse of the azure sea was visible.

"I'll be along soon," March promised. "I just want to look around, see that everything's all right."

"It is, I promise. We've looked in on the place regularly. And do hurry. Miss Emily's been cooking special things for you all day. You look as if you could use some good food."

25

"Oh, what a darling she is. I will, Paulie, I promise."

When the other girl had left her and March had stepped inside the house, the long months of her absence evaporated. She had at once the easy, comfortable feeling of being where she belonged. Paulie and her mother must have done more than merely look in on the house, she thought, for the whole place shone with polishing and dusting, and there were fresh flowers everywhere. March looked around her at the living room with its easy old furniture, bright pillows, its shelves of books and stacks of records. She steeled herself to look at Captain Bobby's small bedroom. The last time she had seen it it had been full of the pain and ominous dread of his illness. But Paulie and Marian Sanders had taken care of that too. The plain spare room had been restored to the way her father had always kept it—the bed neatly made and covered with its brightly colored bedspread. His telescope was in the window, and charts were rolled on the table that stood against one wall.

In her own room there were more fresh flowers, and everything appeared to have been washed, aired, polished. The blue and white flowered curtains looked freshly laundered, her shell collection dusted, the floor with its grass mats neatly swept. March unpacked her suitcase, laying out the new things on her bed. She was startled to find among them a dress she had never seen before. Melissa again! She must have bought it secretly and stuck it in among the other things when March was not looking. She shook her head fondly at such foolishness as she held the dress up. It was a slim white dress made of soft fabric, styled to drape one shoulder and leave one shoulder bare. She would certainly have no occasion to wear anything so grand on Coral Cay. Ah well, she would pack it up and bring it back to New York with her when she returned, and manufacture a small fib to tell Melissa about how much she enjoyed wearing it.

She showered and dressed, hesitating at first about what to wear, and at last, almost shyly, picked out the blue cotton skirt and peasant blouse, and the matching blue espadrilles. She brushed her hair until it shone dark gold in the late afternoon light, then started out the door—but stopped short. There on a hook beside the door, hanging where it had always hung, was her father's hat. His battered old seafaring cap that he had always reached for as he left the house. March stopped still for a moment, trying to quiet the pounding of her heart. Her breath caught. Slowly she reached up and touched the cap, a fond, lingering touch. Then she went out and started hurrying down the path through the pines toward the inn.

CHAPTER 2

IT WAS ONE THING TO TELL PAULIE that no one must dwell on the sadness of Captain Bobby Raffin's death but that they must all remember him fondly and with joy. It was going to be another thing entirely to carry it out, she realized as she stepped into the worn, faintly shabby lobby of the Inn at Coral Cay. There was Paulie's mother Marian, warm and motherly-looking, her eyes sad as she embraced March. And even stocky, balding Don Sanders—Uncle Don, she had called him since she was tiny—his plain friendly face was drawn into lines of concern for her.

I'm going to have to be the one to do it, March thought resolutely. *I'm going to have to set the tone for everybody or none of us will be able to bear it. If only I felt more capable of being strong, of not going to pieces.*

"March, how wonderful to have you back!" Marian Sanders exclaimed, hugging her. "But you look so stylish, so different! Goodness, I'd hardly have known you. Your hair! But you've lost weight, haven't you? Well, Miss Emily can put that to rights." March could tell she was doing her best to sound hearty and cheerful.

"We're all having dinner together," Don Sanders said. "In the family alcove in the dining room."

"Oh, Uncle Don, you're all so busy," March protested. "You don't have to stop everything on my account."

"Now not another word. We want to. We have so much to talk over," he said, and stopped short as if he knew that talking everything over was going to be an emotional ordeal for all of them.

"All right. I'm so happy to be back that I'm not going to argue. But first I have to run out to the kitchen and say hello to Miss Emily."

Tall, statuesque Miss Emily was standing at her big wooden work table slashing at a pile of parsley, mincing it skillfully when March entered the fragrant kitchen. With her coffee-colored skin and her flame-red scarf wrapped around her hair, Miss Emily moved like a queen through her spotless kitchen with its huge ranges, its array of copper pots. She had been at the inn for as long as March could remember. Once years before, March knew, she had worked on Grand Bahama Island in an expensive and fashionable hotel until the day when the owner and a wealthy friend of his had burst into the hotel kitchen, fresh from a day's fishing, and tossed a newly caught fish onto her table. "Cook that up for my friend, Emily," the owner had ordered. Miss Emily had calmly removed her apron. "I am called *Miss* Emily," she said coldly. "And in my kitchen no one tells me what to cook." Some time later she had made her way to Coral Cay and the Sanders' inn, where she had been ever since. No one had ever called her anything but Miss Emily and no one had ever told her what to cook.

Now she murmured, patting March's back, "Captain Bobby's gone, love, but you're back home. You be all right now, back home. And Captain Bobby's only gone in body, not in spirit. You know the kind of faith he had. He always accepted Jesus Christ as his savior. It was what gave meaning to his life." Her voice held a soft and comforting wisdom. Miss Emily knew how important this reminder was to March that death was only a stepping stone to life everlasting.

"Yes, I know, Miss Emily," March murmured. "It's what he taught me too. I'm going to be all right, really."

Back in the dining room she joined the others at a round white-covered table in a small alcove that was always reserved for family, or on rare occasions, special guests. Don Sanders stood up quickly to hold her chair for her; all three faces were taut with anxiety. March sat down and after only a moment's hesitation, said, "Do you remember the widow from Boston?"

Marian Sanders, looking startled, said, "You mean the one who—"

"Yes. The one who came here on a two-weeks' vacation, took one look at Dad and set her cap for him?"

"Chartered the boat every day and had him escort her all around the islands sight-seeing," Paulie chimed in, smiling at the recollection."

"I remember the hamper of food she sent at Christmas time," Don said with slow amusement. "Great huge thing from Filene's or some such place. We all ate preserves and olives and cheese and crackers."

"I remember the tinned shortbread," Marian said. "Delicious! Even Miss Emily said so."

"That was the same year Dad bought the fishing boat, wasn't it?" March asked. "*The Lucky Strike*?"

"I think it was," Don answered. "Now that was a beauty!"

"And remember that professor who'd never been fishing?"

30

"And who must have been the original absent-minded professor—"

"Because a big marlin hit the bait and Dad threw the engine into neutral while someone grabbed the rod—"

"And the professor got so excited he tripped over the fighting chair and went sailing over the side and got tangled in the lines being reeled in—"

Don Sanders leaned over his plate, laughing. Marian Sanders was wiping her eyes and shaking her head at the memory. And across the table Paulie caught March's look and returned it with a smile and a faint nod. We'll be all right now, the look seemed to say. Now that we've let ourselves remember we'll be all right.

Miss Emily came out of the kitchen herself to serve the dinner. "Grouper," she said, putting the first plate in front of March. "Tommy Monday caught it, special for you. I saw him ready to go out bottom-fishing, and I said, don't you come back without a grouper for March."

"Heavenly!" March exclaimed, admiring the fish whose cream-and-orange stripes still showed after delicate broiling in butter. "Miss Emily, there's no one like you!" She had thought her island appetite would never return, but now suddenly she felt a welcome hunger as she watched the table fill up with dishes of rice and brown peas steaming with spice, fresh green salad, carrots with lemon slices and a tangy glaze of sauce. Last of all Miss Emily put in the middle of the table a big bowl which March recognized at once.

"Miss Emily, you made conch! Tommy again?"

Miss Emily nodded. "He went snorkeling for that one. I save you the shell. It's a real pretty one. Good thing I made plenty, too. Somebody else just ask for it, another guest. He even said it right—not like most tourists. He said *conk*, the right way."

March paused with her fork poised over her plate. She had been so preoccupied with the conversation at the table that she had not paid attention to the rest of the dining room, and the alcove where they sat shut them off partially anyway. Now she noticed that the room was filling up with guests, chatting together in low voices and now and then laughing out loud.

"Which guest?" she asked, feeling a disturbing tingle along her spine.

"One over by the window—that one eating alone over there," Miss Emily whispered, and March's eyes followed her nod. The man who had sat beside her in the Cessna was seated at a small table, his back partially turned to them, looking out the window toward the water.

"Know him?" Don Sanders asked.

"No. That is, I sat next to him on the flight from Florida, that's all," March said, turning back quickly, and when she saw them all regarding her curiously she wondered what her face was revealing. She bent to her plate quickly. After a moment she said as casually as she could, "He's staying here then?"

"Yes. Checked in a little before you got here. He'd made a reservation. Name's Simon Wade."

SW, March thought, remembering the monogram on the handkerchief.

"He's a builder—developer, I guess you call them," Don went on. "Specializes in big hotels, resorts, that sort of thing. We talked a little."

March glanced at the man and back at Don. "He's not going to build on here, I hope!"

Don laughed. "That's what I asked him. Wondered if he was going to try to run me out of business. He assured me he wasn't. I guess he's just having himself a holiday here."

Maybe, March thought. But she sensed in Simon Wade a drive and purpose that she did not think lent itself to casual holidays. She rather thought he was a man who did not relax easily. Unless he was meeting a woman here. The one who had been with him on the plane had hinted at that.

"Miss Emily, I haven't tasted anything this good in six months," she said warmly, and gave her attention to her plate. But as she ate, smiled, talked, listened to the well-loved voices around her, she was aware now of the man at the table by the window. His physical presence in the room had an effect on her. Try as she might she could not shut him out of her awareness.

She waited until they were all having their coffee before saying what she knew had to be said—telling them what she had to tell because it would not be fair any other way. They were the people closest to her in the world now, and they had to know. But it was hard to look at them as she spoke, telling them what her plans for the future were. She kept her eyes on her coffee cup. Her fingers traced uneasy patterns on the white tablecloth. When she had said it, when the words were out at last and there was no calling them back, she looked up. Pain and disbelief were on all three faces, but it was Paulie who spoke first.

"March, you can't mean it! Going away from Coral Cay for good?"

Marian's eyes were wide and worried. "But do you really want to, March? Is it what you want?"

March swallowed hard and shook her head. "It doesn't matter what I want," she said huskily. "It's what I have to do."

"But this is your home," Paulie protested. "Your house is here, the boat, all your memories—I mean, do you really think you could live in a big city?"

March's thoughts flew to the city she had left behind her, and the prospect of returning to it for always. To gray streets, unyielding pavements, to waking at the same time each morning and heading for a job inside four walls. To never again hearing the wind whispering in the pine trees, the surf on the rocky shore, crashing and then falling away, never again watching a dark weather front moving in from the west, sending the sea into high combers inside of minutes.

"You won't like it, March, I know you won't," Paulie was protesting, close to tears. "It'll never seem like home to you."

"Now wait, wait," Don Sanders said in his reasonable voice. "If March says she has to do a thing, then there's a reason for it. Let's all stop jumping on her and arguing. Let's hear more about it. What is it, March? What's the real reason?"

March brushed her own tears away and said hopelessly, "I'm broke, Uncle Don. I've used up every cent and I owe people. Six months of hospital bills and doctors—and no income all that time. When you sold the *Lucky Strike* for me this winter, that money was just a drop in the bucket. That's long gone. Even these clothes—my cousin Melissa paid for them."

He said gently, "But you can't possibly earn enough—at least not at first—to do much more than just keep yourself and pay rent."

"No, but if I sell the house and the other boat that'll be a start. Only without the house and boat, how can I stay here?"

"You can live here at the inn with us. You know there's always need for another pair of hands."

March thought of the well-worn carpet in the lobby, the patched table linen and the towels that always seemed to be wearing thin in the middle. "You know I couldn't do that," she said softly. "Even though I love you all. It would be charity, and you know I couldn't do it."

"Just like your old man," Don said despairingly. "Proud and independent."

"But won't you ever come back?" wailed Paulie.

"Oh Paulie, of course I will! I'll have vacations,

34

and of course I'll come here." But to herself she added, *if I can afford the plane fare. And then even if I can, I'll be just another tourist on a two-week holiday in the sun. It won't be home any more. And how will I be able to bear it, seeing someone else living in my little house, someone else walking up that path through the trees?*

"All right now, we've talked enough for one night," Don said firmly. "Time to put the subject away for a while. We still have some thinking to do, and there's no use rushing into anything. If you decide you really have to do this, March, why we'll manage it somehow. It shouldn't be hard to find a buyer for either the house or the boat. But we won't hurry about it. The main object is to get a good price, and you don't do that by grabbing the first offer."

That much at least made sense, March thought, absurdly relieved. "All right," she agreed. "Let's forget about it for now. There's so much else I want to say. Aunt Marian, the house looked beautiful. I know that was your doing—yours and Paulie's."

"Oh, we loved doing it," Marian Sanders said, making an effort at cheerfulness. But her voice drifted off wistfully, and her eyes were still large with worry as they regarded March.

"What about the boat?" March asked Don. "Is it in good shape? Has anyone seen to it while I was away?"

"Seen to it!" Don exclaimed. "Tommy Monday took it on as a personal obligation. He's been working on it ever since you went away—taking it out now and then too. That engine's been tuned up so regularly it's probably able to sing by now. It's not a bad thing to have a master mechanic as an admirer."

"I'm glad," March said. "Because I want to take it out. I was hoping maybe even tomorrow. I'd like to go to the Pines, just for the day."

"Oh March, I'd love to go too," Paulie said. "Only

tomorrow we're expecting that party of school teachers on the early plane and Mom's going to need me. How about the next day?"

"I'll go again when you're free, Paulie," March said quickly. Not for the world would she have hurt Paulie's feelings, but she did long to take this one trip by herself. Whispering Pines Cay, a small, uninhabited island, lay five miles off the leeward beach and could be reached only by careful navigation of dangerous reefs marked by rickety poles—not even buoys or blinkers. It had been Captain Bobby Raffin's favorite spot in the islands – and hence the world— and whenever he could spare time away from the parties of fishermen and tourists that were his livelihood, he and March would set off in the *Flower of the Sea* with one of Miss Emily's lavish lunch hampers and spend the day on Whispering Pines Cay, eating, talking, exploring its three-and-a-half mile length, playing their favorite game of dream-spinning.

"Never saw a place so ideally suited for a hideaway resort," March's father would say, shading his eyes and looking at the offshore breakers that indicated a coral reef.

"But only for a certain type of tourist," March would answer, chiming in with the right response, because they had played this scenario over so many times.

"Right. People who value privacy, who want an unspoiled spot."

"And it has to be done *right*."

"Absolutely. Small scale, careful planning. A few cottages hidden from each other, a marina, a hotel."

"Like Coral Cay only smaller scale."

"And all in the best possible taste. No commercialism."

"Positively none."

At about this point they would open Miss Emily's hamper and sit on the beach, and it never mattered to

36

either of them that the island was owned by someone else—some nameless corporation far away—or that the plan they envisioned would cost millions, and that all they were doing was indulging in dreams. They were good at dreams, both of them, nourished by them. And it did not spoil their pleasure in the least that everything they imagined was impossible of achievement. Their joy was in the imagining. And for the time that they were there, Whispering Pines Cay was their own island.

"Well, fine," Don said now, trying to lift everyone's spirits and return the mood of happy reunion. "Get down to the dock in the morning and Tommy'll fill you in on everything. And no more talk about leaving, not for a while. This is a matter that's going to take some planning and thought."

"All right," March smiled. "We'll forget it for now." But even though she went along with him, she knew it was pretending. There was no way around reality. There it lay like a huge boulder in the pathway, cold and immovable.

When they got up from the table she glanced toward the table at the window, but Simon Wade had left. *At least I know his name now*, March thought. And then quickly, before her thoughts began spinning in that direction, she reminded herself that knowing someone's name was not the same as knowing the person, and that it was highly unlikely she would ever know Simon Wade beyond the chance sharing of a seat on an airplane.

Waking early in the morning to the sound of surf and wind, to the play of shadows on the wall before her was so blissful to March after six months on a convertible couch in Melissa's study-guest room that for a few moments she lay in a drowsy half-doze, opening her eyes now and then to watch the shadows, closing them to shut out everything but the sea and the constant sighing of the island breeze. Then abruptly she remembered her plan for the day and got out of bed, showering quickly and dressing in the jeans and denim shirt she had not worn in so long, tying a red bandana over her hair and hurrying down the path through the woods to the marina.

Early as she was, Tommy Monday was there ahead of her.

"March!" he shouted, and ran to hug her in a bear-like embrace. Tommy had been her friend as long as Paulie. The three of them had walked the island path to school together. He was tall, blond, and muscular, with sun-streaked hair and a powerful build. Today he was in his usual outfit, cutoff jeans and battered sneakers, and his hair had a random look as though he might have forgotten to comb it. "I heard you were home," he said, smiling down at her. Then he grew sober and added, "We felt terrible about the captain when we heard. March, if there's anything I can do. . ."

"Uncle Don tells me you've already done a lot— keeping the boat in good running order."

"Oh, that wasn't anything. I liked doing it. You'll find it's running real great, March. I took it out once a week and I kept the engine sprayed with WD-40. I replaced those old fuel lines, too, so you won't have any more sputtering and cutting out."

"It looks terrific. I might take it out today."

"Great. Want some company?" He studied her face. "No, I guess not. You always did like to get off on your own. Well look, it's all gassed up and ready to go. Only one day soon we'll take a picnic and go out snorkeling, okay?"

"It's a date, Tommy. And thank you for everything."

"I did it because I wanted to. You know that."

"I know. Even so, I do appreciate it." And then, because she did not want to get emotional again, March turned her attention to the boat.

It lay there at the dock, rocking gently at its mooring. It was not new, but its blue hull and white decks gleamed with care and scrubbing. It was a twenty-eight-foot fiberglass boat with a deep V hull— good for slicing through heavy water. Forward there was a small cabin that could sleep two.

"Hey, it's real great to have you home, March," Tommy said softly.

"It's wonderful to be here," she smiled up at him. She did not want to spoil the morning with explanations. Time enough later to tell Tommy she was not home to stay.

"You've got your own key?" She nodded. "Okay. Now I made some adjustments in the steering. You'll find her more responsive than she used to be. May help you when you're steering around those reefs on the way to the Pines." He grinned at her puzzled look. "Now where else would you be headed on your way so early in the morning? Well hey, I'd better get back to the shop. Talk to you later, March."

She watched him stride back along the dock with his easy, athletic step. When he reached the shore he stopped and turned to wave at her before entering the machine shop that adjoined the marina store. She waved back, then jumped lightly down onto the bow of the boat. She felt its easy rocking beneath her and unconsciously her body adjusted to it. It was as if she had never been away. The hard, unyielding sidewalks she had grown used to for the past six months had been more difficult. She had never really become one with them, but now she felt warm again—cradled by the sea, comforted and sustained by it. Would she ever live near the sea this way again? It had been so much a part of her life for so long, all its changing moods and faces familiar to her.

She unsnapped the canvas coverings and stowed them away so that the boat could air out. She checked the safety equipment and the lines, then put up the tall

Bimini top so that she would not get too much sun on her first day back.

"Good morning. I wonder if you could tell me. . ."

March, who had her back to the dock, whirled around and looked up. For a moment the sun was in her eyes, its long low rays making her squint up at the tall figure who stood there. But the voice was one she already knew well. She shaded her eyes with her hand and he came into view more clearly. He was wearing faded jeans and boat shoes that looked well worn. His casual shirt was neatly pressed and crisp.

"I beg your pardon," he said, and the dark shapely eyebrows she remembered arched with surprise as he recognized her. "Mr. Sanders at the inn sent me down here. He said I was to ask for a Mark Raffin, who might agree to take me around the islands today. But if you've already engaged the boat. . ."

March could not help smiling. "It's March, not Mark."

"I beg your pardon?"

"It's March Raffin. That's me."

"You!" For a moment he stared at her in utter bewilderment. Then he dropped down on one knee, his arms resting easily across the other. "Well then. It seems I was mistaken about you. You're not a tourist."

"No."

"This is your home? Coral Cay?"

"Yes, for most of my life." She was amused as she watched him adjust to a new image of her.

"Well then. I apologize."

"For what?"

"For lecturing you on the plane. I must have sounded quite pompous."

"Only a little," March teased.

"Then I'm forgiven?"

March felt warmth stealing into her cheeks. "Yes, of course," she murmured.

He looked out over the water, then back to her and the boat.

"And this belongs to you?" He nodded toward the *Flower of the Sea*.

"Yes."

"Mr. Sanders was correct then in telling me it was a charter boat?"

March hesitated. "It always has been."

"You do the piloting?"

"I can—yes."

He frowned at her. "Why so tentative? You don't sound anxious for business."

"I haven't really been thinking about business much lately, I'm afraid." Why had Don Sanders suggested that she might be willing to let some tourist engage the boat today? She had been thinking ever since yesterday about spending a day at Whispering Pines by herself, with her memories—the last trip, perhaps, that she would ever make there alone. But then at once she realized why. All that talk at the dinner table the night before about her need for money. Don had thought she would welcome a chance to pick up an easy fee for a day's rental of the boat.

A look of impatience crossed his face. "Well, are you interested or aren't you?"

Indecisive women as well as emotional ones seemed to annoy him, March thought. She answered firmly, "Yes, of course. I don't know whether Mr. Sanders mentioned the daily rate to you—"

"I'd be willing to pay three hundred dollars for the day, if that's agreeable to you."

March studied him for a moment. He was obviously a man accustomed to having his own way and willing to pay for it. She knew, too, that many charter boats charged more than the captain had. But something deep inside her, a pride that was perhaps a part of her inheritance from her father, or maybe no more than an inborn island independence, churned up suddenly.

"I was about to say that the price for the day would be a hundred and fifty," she said coolly. "That's more than enough for one passenger."

She could see a small tightening of the muscle in his lean cheek and he stood up quickly. "Very well then. Can we start at once?" His tone had grown distant, impersonal.

"Certainly. We may need to take some food if it's to be a long day."

"I've already thought of that. The kitchen at the inn was kind enough to prepare a hamper. I'll get it." He strode back along the dock to where he had left a basket. March stared after him. The inn's kitchen meant Miss Emily, and Miss Emily always required advance notice about picnics. She was known to be highly intolerant of guests who breezed in at the last minute and asked her to knock together "a little something." A large tip, possibly, had been the inducement, but somehow March thought not. Miss Emily had very stubborn pride.

He returned with the hamper, handed it down to her and then slid down onto the small forward deck where March stood. The *Flower of the Sea* rolled gently, accommodating itself to the new weight, and March shifted lightly with the roll. A feeling of excitement and uncertainty that had nothing to do with the movement of the boat seemed to move upward from her toes until she could feel it flowing along her legs and arms and settling in an odd way somewhere around her midsection. She had felt it before, as she boarded the small plane in Florida with him directly behind her. Something about his masculinity, his very presence so near her, seemed to produce a magnetism that drew her to him. At the same time she was aware of a tingling sense of danger that such power implied. She tried to keep her voice brisk and businesslike.

"If you stow that in the forward cabin it'll be out of the sun. Then if you don't mind casting off that stern line I'll take care of the bow."

He moved under the Bimini top, tucked the hamper out of sight, and went aft at once to loosen the stern line, doing it all with easy, well-coordinated movements and without a trace of hesitation. March cast off the bow line and opened the engine cover to let out any accumulation of hazardous fumes, then started the engine and maneuvered the boat carefully away from the dock. Without being told, he stood ready with a boat hook to fend off in case the boat swung about, but March guided it skillfully into open water.

"Was there some particular place you wished to see?" she asked. "There are any number of points of interest around here." She had raised her voice a little to be heard over the noise of the engine and the wind that swept past them. When she turned to him, she found to her surprise that he was looking, not out over the water but at her, studying her as she stood there in the pilot's spot behind the wheel, the wind pressing her blue denim shirt against the curves of her slender body. It was a look frankly curious and holding another element that she could not at the moment define. There was a glittering light in the oddly shaped eyes, and the broad, well-formed mouth looked almost ready to smile. March turned away from him quickly as though to keep track of her course. "Oh, and by the way," she went on, speaking rapidly to cover a strange inner confusion she was feeling, "I forgot to ask you. Are you a strong swimmer? Because if not, you should be wearing a life preserver. They're in the cabin there where you put the hamper, and we always urge anyone who's not—"

"I'm sure I'll be quite safe," he said. "I'm not unaccustomed to the water."

She gave him a sidelong glance, remembering her first impression of him as having a swimmer's long lean build. "Just as you say. I felt I should ask. Now, as to where you'd like to go—"

"So you do this for a living?" he asked suddenly.

March felt speechless, unable, for the moment, to answer. Six months ago she would have answered yes—promptly, happily. Now the question only made her more than ever aware of the limbo in which she was existing. She was living in a strange hollow world of transition where nothing was defined. And even though she had felt comfortable and warm and contented at being back on Coral Cay, she knew that she no longer belonged here. She was here only to tie up loose ends, say her farewells. Did she do this for a living? Not really. Not any longer.

"My father did, for many years. This boat was his," she said. "Most of the people here make their living from the sea one way or another." It was a vague answer that told him nothing, she thought. But then, who was he to inquire into her life? A stranger, nothing more, and she had no wish to share intimate details about herself with a stranger.

"I see." His flat tone of voice indicated that he realized he was being rebuffed. "Well then, as to where we're going, I presume you know all the routes well? Among the islands, that is?"

"Yes, of course."

"The place I want to go is not far from Coral Cay. It's called Whispering Pines Cay. It lies almost due north, I believe. You're acquainted with it? I know the navigation is a bit tricky."

March turned to stare at him. He was standing beside her now, holding the top of the windshield and looking out over the water. The wind was ruffling his dark hair, blowing it back from his forehead.

"Whispering Pines Cay!" she exclaimed. "How on earth do you know about that? Nobody goes there." *Nobody but us*, she thought with a stab of pain around her heart. *Nobody but Captain Bobby and me*.

Now it was his turn to deflect her question, to answer evasively. "I've heard a good bit about it," he said. "Do you know the route?"

"Yes, of course, but—"

"Is there some reason why you don't want to take me there?" He had turned to face her once more and his features had taken on an impatient look. The mouth was pressed into a line of annoyance, drawing it down slightly at the corners. The dark eyes were narrowed. "I understand it's a place only experienced pilots care to go. If you feel it's beyond you, it's quite all right. I'll find someone else."

Anger and pride flared up in March, crowding out, for the moment, all the softer emotions. "I know the route well," she said, and color blazed in her cheeks. "I'll be happy to take you there." He was still looking at her in that narrow, appraising way, and she could not help adding, "You'll be perfectly safe in the *Flower of the Sea*, I promise you."

His features relaxed into a faintly supercilious look. "Fine," he said quietly. "Can't ask for more than that."

March turned away from him brusquely and gave her attention to the ship-to-shore radio. Simon Wade, apparently interested in the mechanics of the operation, inquired, "Routine radio check, I suppose?"

"Yes, we have to monitor Channel Sixteen every time we leave port. Just to be sure they're reading us and we're able to read them." She flipped on the switch and picked up the telephone receiver. "Coral Cay Marina, Coral Cay Marina. This is the *Flower of the Sea* requesting a radio check. Over."

A voice came back, crackling but quite clear. "*Flower of the Sea*, this is Coral Cay Marina. We're reading you loud and clear. Over."

"Coral Cay Marina, this is the *Flower of the Sea*. Thank you. over and out." She replaced the receiver. "Now if someone is trying to reach us we know we'll hear it."

"That's a monitoring channel, I take it."

"Yes. We have to switch to a different one to have

45

a conversation with another craft. Sixteen is strictly for raising your party, or for a call for help, naturally.'' She had the impression that he stored away every bit of information, no matter how small, that every detail interested him. *As long as we stay on subjects like that we'll be able to get through the day*, she thought, easing the boat out of the shelter of the marina and northeastward around Rocky Point, the farthest tip of Coral Cay. Once around the point she changed to a westward course, keeping Coral Cay on their left so that they could see its wooded slopes spreading down toward rocky beaches, all the trees darkly green and looking like a solid mass of vegetation. Simon Wade was silent at her side until suddenly the first pole with a faded red rag tied to it showed above the waves on their starboard side.

''Reefs?'' he asked sharply.

She nodded, and now gave all her attention to navigating. As familiar as every reef was to her, she never dared let down her guard. Captain Bobby Raffin had drummed the lesson into her over and over—the first rule of the sea. ''Never close your eyes to the sea, my girl. And never turn you back on it. It can snap back at you as fast as a cat with a mouse.'' Yet he always added, ''Only remember this too. You're never alone out there. In the roughest sea, in the strongest wind, Someone is watching over you. Our Lord Jesus never forgets us, March.'' Now, concentrating on her course, March wondered whether the man beside her was questioning her ability, wondered, too, whether perhaps he would have been happier if his charter captain had really been Mark Raffin instead of March. She would not take her eyes from the course to look at him, but she could feel that he had not moved from his position at her side. When they had passed the first of the reefs she let her breath out in a small puff that she was sure was not audible over the wind's rush.

"Very nicely done, Captain," Simon Wade said, and he sounded relaxed. If he had been nervous about her navigating he at least kept it out of his voice.

"Thank you," she said crisply. And then she added, "There are more reefs up ahead, of course."

How true that was, she thought.

CHAPTER 3

THEY APPROACHED THE ISLAND from southwest, dropping anchor in the sheltered cove where the curving arm of silvery beach provided protection.

"We may get a little wet," she said, but he seemed unconcerned and was in fact already rolling up his jeans and scuffing off his shoes. He slipped over the side gracefully and then took the picnic hamper she handed him, while she followed carrying their shoes. As they waded toward shore she watched the play of muscles in his back and shoulders as he carried the basket over his head, native-style. There was a strong, graceful look about everything he did, she thought. March found herself staring at his back in wordless fascination, growing more and more aware of the maleness of him, the nearness, and the power. It was the same reaction she had felt before, but each time she became aware of it, it seemed to have increased in intensity until now, quite suddenly, she felt a touch of fear along with it, as though a fascination so strong carried with it a hint of danger. But what sort of danger? And what was she afraid of?

She felt a need to break the silence, as though there might be some safety in conversation.

"This sandy beach is quite rare," she said abruptly. "Usually the beaches around here are rocky. Of course it's a narrow one. And actually, this is the only safe landing on the island. Further along, toward Solitude Point, it's quite rocky again and there are dangerous reefs. The point itself can only be reached on foot. You might like to see it though. It's very beautiful."

"I would," he answered.

"It's odd that you should even know about this island," she said. "Most outsiders don't."

He did not answer, and she felt embarrassed at having seemed to pry. But then they reached the shore and he put the hamper down and looked around. Following him, March stumbled and at once recovered her balance, but not before his hand had come out to steady her. His touch was so startling that she drew back as though she had felt fire. *And have I?* she wondered in confusion. *Am I about to be burned, one way or another?*

He seemed unaware of her confusion. He stood on the sandy strip, once again surveying the landscape, turning to take it in from every direction, and it seemed to March there was an appraising expression on his face—eyes narrowed to concentration, mouth pursed as though in speculation.

"Is this the only approach to the island?" he asked abruptly. "The way we came?"

"No, it can be approached from the west or north. The way we came is the safest, as long as you're with somebody who knows it well," she said.

"Which I certainly was," he said, smiling down at her suddenly. It seemed to her the smile was so dazzling that for the moment she turned her head away as though from strong sunlight. *I must be careful*, March thought nervously. *There is something*

49

dangerous about this man. He is too used to having his own way.

But in spite of her cautious resolve, his next words disarmed her completely. "This is the most beautiful place I've ever seen. You must show me everything. Which way first?"

For a moment March hesitated, standing there on the narrow strip of sand with the tall stranger. The wind off the water blew at her; she slipped her bandana off and let her hair blow forward over her cheeks and curl around her ears. Behind them, the sapphire sea lapped curling over the white sandy beach. All around them the oleanders and palms stirred and whispered. What danger could possibly lie in such a bright and beautiful morning? He stood there, still looking down at her and waiting, and after a moment he said, "Well then? Lead on Captain March."

March came to with a start and tried to ignore the mocking twinkle in his eye. She was a charter boat captain with a fare, she reminded herself, being paid to escort a tourist on an island outing. There was no more to it than that. And if this business of exploring Whispering Pines Cay was a little outside a usual day's routine for a charter boat—why, what of it? She was being well compensated for the service, and it was all strictly business.

She said briskly, "Let's put the hamper somewhere in the shade and then start looking around. There's a little path through the trees over that way." She pointed. "It leads up toward a lovely grassy plateau that slopes down toward the sea on the northern side. You'd better put your shoes back on. We'll be doing a lot of walking." She waited while he slipped into the worn deck shoes and deposited the lunch hamper under a small cluster of trees at the edge of the beach. Then, as they started along the upward-sloping path that led through a fringe of palms and away from the shore, she said, "The island is about three and a half miles long. At its widest point, about a mile across. To the north lies another larger island, and that shelters it—protects it from the north winds blowing in off the Atlantic. That protection has kept its shoreline from eroding, kept those great crashing waves away from it. If you've seen any of the craggy rocky shores on some the outlying islands you can see how they've been eaten away."

"Strange for such an ideal spot to be totally uninhabited, isn't it?" he asked, following along behind her on the narrow path. March kept her eyes on the way ahead, although she was acutely conscious of the measured sound of his long stride at her back. But she was doing it right, she told herself, striking just the right impersonal guidebook note.

"In a way. But the reefs have always protected it. Even fishermen don't care for them, and since there are so many good places to fish around the islands, why look for difficult ones? Also, navigating among these smaller islands in the Bahamas can be pretty bewildering in other ways."

"How do you mean?"

"Guidebooks and charts aren't updated very often. A chart that tells you to look for a prominent house on the south end of an island, for example, might have been written ten years ago. Today that house might be overgrown with vegetation and almost impossible to pick out from a boat. So unless you really know the waters—"

"I see."

"Oh, picnickers come here now and then, and I guess occasional campers. Not many, though. For the same reason. With so many easily accessible places, why look for dangerous ones?"

"It must be a challenge to some, though," he said thoughtfully. "There are always people like that—the ones who want to climb Everest and so on."

"Oh yes. There have been those," she admitted. "I'll tell you more about that later." She sought about anxiously for more information that would keep her on a tour guide footing. "The vegetation here is very much like that of the rest of the islands, you'll notice. The Australian pine is the commonest." She pulled at a low needled branch and said, "You see? The needles are like your Scotch pine, but the trees themselves haven't such a regular shape. I suppose because of the constant wind. They're softer, frailer-looking. And you see how they bend with the wind? Most of the natives think they're a nuisance, but I've always loved them."

"Very beautiful," he said at her back, speaking in a low tone that sounded somehow intimate. March, hearing the sound, quickened her stride.

"The palms are various sorts—coconut, Kentia, windmill. The oleanders – you saw those down near the beach as well—they grow quite huge here, fifteen to twenty feet. I've always wondered whether they seeded themselves here or whether someone planted them on this island once long ago. The flowers are various shades of rose, pink, and of course white. But poisonous, you know. All parts of the plant, so they're to be looked at only."

"Ah, I see. A deadly beauty, one might almost say. I've heard there are women like that."

March swallowed nervously and ignored the jibe. "Hibiscus is smaller," she said firmly. "That's hibiscus over there." She pointed to masses of yellow and red blossoms. The sloping path leveled off and the trees around them thinned as they approached the grassy plateau. March pointed across the windswept clearing. "Over there's the place where it's the widest, just about opposite where we're standing. From the shore over there you can glimpse the island to the north, the one I told you about. There are more woods on our left, but not dense ones. Very pretty, actually, and a lot of sunlight comes through. To the right is the way we'll walk if you want to see Solitude Point. It's a good two miles, but if you don't mind that—"

"I don't mind," he said. He stood beside her in the clearing with the sunlight behind him so that all March was aware of was his tall looming shape, the broad shoulders and the dark curly hair caught and highlighted by the sun. She could feel a quickening of her pulse, a hammering that was so loud in her ears she thought he must hear it, too.

Suddenly he said in a quiet voice, "Why were you crying on the plane?"

She was so startled she gave a little gasp and turned quickly away from him. "That's none of your—I mean, it was just something personal—something—" Her voice quavered and broke off and to her chagrin she felt her eyes filling with tears again. Gently he put both hands on her shoulders and turned her to face him.

"What was it?" he said, still in that soft tone.

It seemed to spill out without her willing it. "I had just—said goodbye to someone," she murmured thickly.

"Ah." He sounded thoughtful. The hands that held her shoulders were warm. His touch burned through her denim shirt. "Someone you loved."

"Yes. Someone I loved." *What is making me do this?* March wailed silently to herself. *I was so brave with Paulie and her parents, with Melissa and Bill— with everyone else.*

"And will you never see this person again?"

"No, never. Not in this life."

"Ah well, once an affair is truly over—"

She saw with dismay that he had the wrong idea completely.

"Oh, but you see, it wasn't a love affair, nothing like that. It was my father. He was ill and I took him

53

to New York for treatment. He was in the hospital there for six months before he died. He was all the close family I had."

"I see," he said, and then for a moment he was silent, studying her face. She thought that any minute he would start saying all those sympathetic things people say, and she wouldn't be able to bear it—not again. But all he said, in a quiet voice, was, "I suspect then that he was the one who taught you to handle a boat so well. And to steer around those reefs."

March, realizing that she was holding her breath tensely, let it out in a gentle sigh of relief. How had he known exactly the right thing to say? "Yes, that's true," she said softly. "He was a charter boat captain and a very fine sailor. Everyone called him Captain Bobby. We had a very good life here."

"Had?" He seemed to have a way of catching every nuance in what she said. "But you're home again now, and surely it's still a good life."

"Yes, well, for now."

He asked curiously. "What did you mean before when you said, 'Not in this life'?"

March looked into his eyes. "Why, simply that in the life everlasting we will meet again, of course."

She saw one eyebrow shoot up. "Of course? That sounds like a very firm conviction."

"Yes, it is," March said quietly.

"I see." His broad shoulders lifted in a shrug. "Well, for those who believe in it—"

"You don't, I take it?"

"I've never given it much thought."

She moved away from him, out from under the strong hands on her shoulders. There was more she could have said, out of an overflowing heart, but he was, after all, a stranger. She had already said more than she had intended. And she did not want him to misinterpret. Sympathetic though he was, she did not want him to think she was adding her name to the list of clinging dependent females trailing in his wake. The beautiful Diana who had been with him on the plane, the unknown Penny who, she gathered, might be coming here to meet him. Women seemed to gravitate toward him, to draw from his strength, she suspected. *But I must find my own strength, she thought firmly. I'm not going to borrow from anyone.* She brushed her tears away hastily and stood a few paces apart from him. She lifted her chin and asked, "What would you like to see first?"

For the rest of the day they tramped over the little island, exploring every grove and slope and clearing. They ate their lunch on the narrow beach and listened to the soothing repetitious voice of the waves against the shoreline and watched the *Flower of the Sea* bobbing at anchor in the peaceful cove. At Solitude Point, the high bluff that was the southeastern tip of the island, they took off their shoes and sat in the grass looking down on the rocky shore below them.

"Remember my saying I would tell you more about some of those who took the island on as a challenge?" she said, pointing down toward the jagged rocks. "There's evidence of it down there." He followed her pointing finger down to where the stern of a wrecked sailboat lay shattered on the rocks. "Shall we go down for a look?"

"I told you I wanted to see it all."

They slipped into their shoes again and he got up, reaching down to help her up. This time her hesitation was brief. It was a long time since she had had such a wonderful day. Was there any harm in enjoying it, and him, even though she knew it to be no more than an interlude, a day that would never be repeated? She put her own hand in his and felt the long flexible fingers grasping hers, felt his strength as he pulled her effortlessly to her feet. Together they scrambled down the bank and onto the wet gray rocks that stood like bulwarks against the sea. Beyond them, ripples of white water indicated the presence of the deadly reefs. Still visible on the shattered stern of the skeleton boat was its name: *Dream Come True*.

"Sobering reminder," he murmured. "Someone should break it up and burn it."

"Except that it's rather beautiful, in a way. Like bleached bones. And then too—"

"What?"

"Well, it's sort of a reminder, as you say."

"Of Mother Nature's whims?"

"Yes. A warning not to take her too lightly."

He looked down at her with a strange intensity, studying her face. His dark uptilted eyes seemed to bore deep, to penetrate to places where her most secret thoughts were hidden. She felt once again the need to keep talking, as though talk might create a barrier that would protect her from his scrutiny.

"There are always people who have a way of spoiling whatever they touch, who feel they have to rearrange nature."

"And this island. You'd like to keep it as your own private preserve. No one else should be able to enjoy it but you."

His mouth had taken on a sardonic, one-sided twist. March said with quick defensiveness, "Certainly not. Not at all."

"You told me earlier you'd lived here most of your life."

"Yes."

"Then you weren't born here?"

"Oh no. I'm an American."

"You are?"

"Is that so surprising?"

"Well, somehow I thought . . . you seem so at home here."

"I was born in the United States, in a little town on the Gulf coast of Florida. Always lived near water, you see. But when my mother died—I was two

56

then—my father and I came here to visit. Uncle Don Sanders and my father were old friends. It was supposed to be only a short stay, but somehow my father could never bring himself to go back. I think it would have been so painful for him to go back to where he had been happy with her. So anyway, he bought a boat and began a small business with it, and then there was a house vacant, and it seemed natural for us to move in. . .and. . ." March shrugged, looking up at him.

"You just stayed on."

"Yes. I suppose it was partly on my account too. Because I had Aunt Marian, who always treated me the same as Paulie. And there was Paulie herself, to be like a sister to me."

He said with amusement, "I guess I took you for a native because you seemed so huffy about outsiders coming in and changing things."

"I didn't know I was being huffy."

"Oh, decidedly," he smiled.

"What changes are we talking about anyway?" Once again she felt him probing her thoughts.

He studied her curiously for a moment. The wind sweeping in off the water was driving the dark gold hair around her face. She reached up with one hand to push it back. "What changes?" she repeated.

"Let's walk back up," he said, and again reached out with his hand. This time she took it almost without thinking, her mind going in other directions as she scrambled up the slope with him. At the top he let go her hand and put both his own hands on his lean hips. His head tilted to one side as he regarded her. "Do you know what I do for a living?" he asked. A quizzical smile played around the corners of his mouth.

"Uncle Don—Mr. Sanders—said you were a builder. A developer, I think he called it."

"Yes. Well, actually I'm a designer-contractor. I

take on commissions to design and build things—or my company does. Mostly resort hotels and condominiums. You're familiar with the Bel-Surf Hotel in Palm Beach?"

"I've seen pictures of it," she said, trying to sound noncommittal as she recalled a great concrete-and-glass structure dominating the shoreline. It had been featured in a dozen glossy magazines at the time of its opening. Movie stars had arrived in Maseratis and a senator had cut a ribbon.

"You don't approve, I see." There was a glint of amusement in the dark eyes.

"It's not for me to approve or disapprove," she said stiffly. "It's none of my business, is it?"

"But you do think it's garish and vulgar," he persisted. "I imagine that's your assessment of my work."

"Really, it's none of my business," she repeated, "only—" She paused and then some perverse nudging made her add, "I can see why you'd like to get away from it now and then and come on a holiday to a place like this."

He laughed out loud. "Spoken like a true islander," he declared. "Unfortunately it's not quite accurate. I'm not here as a tourist. I'm in Coral Cay on business."

March frowned. "Business? On our little backwater island? Besides, Uncle Don asked you if you were planning on building on Coral Cay and you told him no."

"I didn't know I'd been discussed," he said blandly. "However, Coral Cay isn't the place I'm interested in. It's this island—Whispering Pines."

A chill ran through March's whole body in spite of the bright sun that was shining down on them out of cloudless blue.

"What sort of business?" she whispered. But deep inside she already knew with a grim cold sureness.

"It's to be developed as a resort," he said in an offhanded way.

The sunlight turned to blackness and spinning shapes as a chilly paralysis gripped March. For a moment the enormity of what he was saying held no reality. Instead, memories came flooding over her—images of all those long afternoons she and her father had spent tramping the island, picnicking on its shores, spinning dreams. Making Whispering Pines into their own kind of resort in their imaginations. Building the small tucked-away cottages, the simple marina, the modest inn that would blend into the landscape, constructing a future out of dreams. But reality stood before her in the shape of this tall man—all plans and assessments. All market research and cost accounting. And yes, she supposed grudgingly, all talent and ability, too.

"Developed?" she asked at last in a small voice. "Your company's to do it?"

"Yes. I'm here to look the place over—make some preliminary maps and sketches."

"But it's so hidden away, so hard to reach. Who would ever come here? And how? Surely there's no room for a landing field."

"Well, no. But I'm sure a helicopter pad could be fitted onto that plateau, although it may not be needed. In spite of the difficulty of getting here, the harbor itself is good. Deep water and a sheltered spot. Larger boats might be able to approach from the other direction. Open sea that way, of course, but large-sized boats wouldn't object to that."

"Yachts, you mean," she said weakly.

"Well yes, perhaps. This resort would be for a very special sort of clientele."

"Money, I suppose."

"That's only one element. People of particular tastes, I should say."

March fell silent as she thought of Whispering Pines

Cay turned into a haven for the wealthy, the free-spending, the bored, the novelty-seeking, its shoreline defiled by high-rises, its grassy open spaces dotted with tennis courts and driving ranges. No doubt there would be a casino and bright, smart shops. But all very small and exclusive, she thought bitterly, so that in no time it would become a trendy, prestigious place to vacation. It would find its way into the columns of newspapers. A film star or two would take it up and in time the whole gaping world would find its way there.

She turned away from him and walked a few steps away, hugging herself as though from cold and looking out over the sea. She could feel him coming up behind her.

"That upsets you, doesn't it?" he asked in a low voice.

"It's nothing to me," she answered coldly. "I don't own the island."

"You act as if you did."

"I don't act that way at all," she stormed, still looking away from him. "It's just that people like you—"

"People like me?" he interrupted. "You haven't the faintest idea what sort of person I am."

"Oh, yes, I do. People who can never leave well enough alone, who have to spoil everything they touch. People who like to rearrange nature for profit."

"And you'd rather have this place as your own private hideaway, is that it? No one else should be able to see or enjoy it but you?"

"That's not what I mean. But there are all kinds of ways to treat a place. And the one thing that would ruin this island is your kind of building."

"Big, glossy, and vulgar?" he said mockingly.

"Those are your words, not mine," she snapped. "But you do seem to have sized up your own work pretty accurately." She paused and took a deep breath, and suddenly a black depression swept over

60

her. *Why should I care?* she asked herself wearily. *What difference will it make to me?* Indeed, she would be far away from the islands by the time he started moving in his big barges and their freight of heavy machinery, of earth-moving equipment. By the time they started slicing into the landscape, carving up the island and rearranging its delicate beauty, she would be a world away. *Only after it's done I will never come here again—never,* she told herself. *I wouldn't be able to bear it.*

She felt his hands resting on her shoulders again and his head bent down so that his mouth was close to her ear.

"And just when I thought we were getting on so well," he murmured.

She whirled around to face him angrily. "I can't imagine what you mean, Mr. Wade. If you think—"

"Couldn't you call me Simon?" he asked, and there was a teasing note in his voice.

"Certainly not," she protested, taking a backward step. "I brought you here for the day because you're paying me to do it. That's all there is to our relationship."

"And all there is behind you is a rather steep drop," he said with amusement, and reaching out, he put both hands on her waist and pulled her to him. His head bent down to come between her and the blinding afternoon sun as his mouth closed over hers. He held he so close that she could feel the hard, muscular body all along the length of her own, could hear a pounding, hammering beat that was someone's heart—*mine or his?* she thought in a kind of terror. But it was not terror of him, only of herself, she realized. *Am I so vulnerable then? Am I going to be prey to the first handsome man who touches me? And this man above all—this man who plays on women's emotions as an experienced musician upon his instrument?* But then the pounding grew louder and the burst of golden sunlight around his dark head a blinding nimbus that shut out all other thoughts except his presence, and the sun-warmed lips that were enveloping hers. For a moment the two of them stood locked together on the high grassy bluff with the sea wind swirling around them, *as though we were the first two people in the world*, March thought in wonder. Then reality and the present came spinning back, and she pulled away from him.

"You've made a mistake, Mr. Wade," she gasped breathlessly. "Only my boat is for hire. I am not."

His smile as he looked down at her was mocking again.

"I see. That sturdy island independence again, eh? Well, far be it from me to take advantage of a guest."

"A guest!"

"Yes. I thought you'd have figured it out by now. This is my island you're on. I own it."

"But I thought—aren't you doing this resort as a commission for someone—some company? I understood the island was owned by a corporation somewhere."

"Was, yes. However, this is one project I'm doing on my own, for myself. I bought your island a week ago, Captain March."

CHAPTER 4

MARCH AWOKE THE NEXT MORNING with none of the feelings of comfort and belonging that she had experienced on the previous morning. The sun slanted through the window in the same way, made the same moving patterns on the wall. The wind ruffled the blue and white curtains in the same way, promising another beautiful day. Why then was her heart so heavy, and why did she have vague feelings of regret about something? She shut her eyes tight and memory surged back as the events of the day before returned to her. She buried her face in her pillow, but the memory refused to be shut out. It was really true. Whispering Pines—*her* island—was to be destroyed. It was all settled, all beyond her control. There was nothing she could do about it.

A small voice deep inside her nudged at her, trying to make itself heard. March ignored it, but it would not be silent. *Is that really what's bothering you?* the voice asked. *Or is it that kiss at Solitude Point?* At the thought of it March felt again the tingling excitement sweeping along her arms and legs and churning up inside her. A blush of color flared in her cheeks. *I will not think about him*, she told herself firmly. *I absolutely refuse to think of him. He is a man who likes to control women, who likes knowing he can have any woman he wants. I will not add myself to the list.*

Holding tight to the thought, she jumped out of bed, slipped out of her pale pink, cotton night gown and hurried to dress, putting on a red and white striped T-shirt, a faded, disreputable pair of blue jeans and the old deck shoes she wore for hard work. Keeping busy was the best way to keep her mind off her own misery. There's nothing like work to make the world look better, her father had always said, and March knew it was true, but she thought she would have a hard time proving it today. She paused in front of her mirror long enough to run a brush through her hair and then tied her red bandana tightly over her curls, yanking at the ends of the tie with special severity.

Walking down the piney path toward the inn she tried to think more calmly about what she had learned yesterday and to cheer herself a little. The Bahamian government moved slowly at best—she was quite sure of that. Their approval would certainly be required for a job as big as the one Simon Wade was planning. Approval might take months. By that time perhaps he would grow tired of the waiting and the red tape. Some other big job might beckon, something lucrative on the other side of the world. But then— March stopped still in the path– she would never see him again, would she? She was angry with herself at the quick way *that* had popped into her head. Wasn't that exactly what she wanted, after all? To be rid of him? She resumed walking, more quickly now, and veered from the path to go directly to the back kitchen door of the inn.

Paulie was sitting at the big wooden work table having breakfast and chatting with Miss Emily as the latter moved about effortlessly preparing breakfasts for guests who were up early.

"Hi, everybody," March said. "I seem to have misplaced my scrub bucket. And could I borrow some cleanser?"

"Well, some greeting!" Paulie complained good-naturedly. "Are you going to wash that boat again? It's already the cleanest one at the marina. Tommy's seen to that."

"I'd like to keep busy," March said, ignoring the knowing glance that Paulie cast in her direction.

"You sit down and have some breakfast," Miss Emily said sternly, breaking an egg into a pan and pouring a cup of coffee with smooth easy motions and a firmness that did not allow for argument.

"Oh, I really don't think I'll bother—" March began, but Paulie grinned at her. "You might as well argue with the tide, March, you ought to know that. Sit down and give in gracefully." As March took a seat opposite her she added, "I hear you didn't get to take your solitary trip to Whispering Pines after all yesterday."

"No. Your dad sent me a customer. Imagine that, on my first day back. So I made myself a day's charter fare. That was a bit of luck, wasn't it?" She suspected that her false cheerfulness was not fooling Paulie, but she had no wish to go over yesterday's events with anyone just yet. The whole subject was still too painful.

"He's terribly good-looking, isn't he?" Paulie said, eyes sparkling. "We certainly don't get many like him as hotel guests."

"Mm. I guess. I was paying attention to my navigating."

Paulie, who knew her well enough to read her signals, did not ask her any more questions, and when Miss Emily slid a plate in front of her March ate quickly, not giving her usual appreciation to an egg that had been prepared as a work of art. She finished her coffee, rummaged in the broom closet for a scrub bucket and cleanser, and started out the door.

"Thanks, Miss Emily." She paused, thinking she had been a little too uncommunicative, and said, "What are you doing for lunch, Paulie?"

"Meeting you, at one o'clock?" Paulie laughed.

"Good. See you then."

"Oh March," Paulie called after her as she started out. "Big cruiser coming in today. I heard them radio in for a slip at the marina first thing this morning."

March waved to signal she had heard but was already headed down the path toward the marina. She could hear the familiar boating sounds—engines starting up, rigging clanging against the masts of sailboats. The start of another busy day. She saw the forty-foot Hatteras from North Carolina that had pulled in the day before just leaving its slip for a day of deep-sea fishing. In the next slip was a twenty-five-foot Mako, a boat made to accommodate divers and to negotiate the treacherous coral reefs. Between the Mako and the *Flower of the Sea* was a large empty slip—no doubt reserved for the cruiser Paulie had mentioned.

March hopped aboard her boat, unsnapped the coverings and stowed them neatly in the cabin. She collected the brushes and sponges she would need for cleaning and the special oils she would apply to the teak rim when the cleaning was done. Her father had been very particular about the care of the boat, one of the reasons, she knew, that Don Sanders now assured her it would be easy to sell.

March scrubbed and scrubbed the already nearly spotless boat until it gleamed with a dazzling brightness. She was rinsing the soapy water from the rear deck when a sixty-foot custom-made Burger cabin cruiser made its way slowly into the marina. It turned hard to port when it passed the first dock and

March saw that it was indeed headed for the slip next to hers. It maneuvered easily into position at the empty slip. *An advantage of twin propellers*, March thought. Two propellers enabled even large boats to negotiate tight places gracefully. The stern of the big boat faced the *Flower of the Sea* so March could read its name clearly: the *Ayes of Texas* hailing from Houston. March had seen such boats many times at the marina and could visualize its occupants even before they came ashore. They would be well groomed with that studied casual appearance that came from shopping at the most expensive stores. The passengers aboard this one did not disappoint her. No sooner had the crew fastened the lines securely to the pilings of the dock than a girl of twenty or so appeared from inside the cabin.

March saw that she was tall, five feet seven or eight, with long blonde hair that she wore in a single braid down the middle of her back. She was dressed entirely in pale yellow—a soft silky blouse tied at her nicely tanned midriff, neatly creased shorts, and sandals with straps so thin March thought they would surely break at the first step. The only jewelry she wore was a pair of diamond stud earrings that sent off sparks of white fire in the hot midday sun. The girl looked around her as if to get her bearings and then stepped easily from the boat to the dock. For a moment she stood there examining her surroundings with what looked to March like bored indifference. Then she turned back to the boat and called out, "Are you coming, Monica? I am absolutely dying to stretch my legs!" The boredom was in her voice, March thought, as well as a note of petulance. *She's a girl who's used to having her own way*, no mistaking that. Somehow it came as a surprise to March, who could never remember being bored. She suddenly realized that she was staring and that water running from the hose was forming a pool around her feet. She stepped up onto the dock and turned the water off, neatly coiled the hose and returned it to its proper place. She was standing quite close to the girl now and although the newcomer was taking no notice of her March felt awkward about not speaking. Boat people always spoke to each other. So, in spite of her drowned-rat appearance, she smiled and said, "Hi. I'm March Raffin. Is this your first time on the island?"

The blonde girl turned to her slowly and March felt herself being examined from head to toe. It was hard to read the girl's expression because her eyes were covered by a pair of oversized sunglasses with the rhinestone initials CM in the lower corner of one huge lens.

"Caitlin Massie. Yes, it is," she responded coolly. Then deliberately, she turned away and called again, "Monica! *Are* you coming?"

A second woman appeared from the yacht's cabin.

"Honestly, Caty honey! I'm coming!" She was older than Caitlin Massie, March saw, and her blonde hair was not the natural silky blonde of the girl's. Rather it was streaked and frosted and done in the latest shoulder-length frizzy style that March knew was fashionable from her afternoon at Rene's in New York. She was wearing a lavender velour one-piece jumpsuit—strapless and with very short shorts—the kind of thing most women would wear over a bathing suit. Her lavender high-heeled slip-on sandals were the only other clothing she wore. There were several gold chains around her neck and on her hand the biggest diamond March had ever seen. She made her way toward them cautiously, watching her step and concentrating on the hazardous high heels, talking all the way.

"Honestly, Caty honey! You just barely give me time to get dressed and get my makeup on, and what's the *rush* ? Your daddy says we're going to be here a week or two, and that's sure plenty of time to see everything. I mean, if it were Freeport or one of those places, there might be some reason—" She paused and in a quick glance took in the weathered marina, the modest inn. "Oh, my *word*. Is this *it*? I am going to have to speak to your daddy. There must be someplace else he can fish." She stepped gingerly onto the dock and now saw March standing next to Caitlin. "Why, Caty, I didn't know you'd made a friend already—now where are your manners, girl?"

But something had taken Caitlin Massie's attention on shore at the end of the dock. Without looking at the woman or at March she said vaguely, "Oh. This is my stepmother, Monica Massie. Monica, this is Marge—what did you say your last name was?" She waved a hand in an indifferent gesture of introduction and went on looking toward shore.

"Raffin. And it's March—like the month." No one said anything, and March felt compelled to add, "I own the *Flower of the Sea*. I'm docked next to you." Caitlin did not react, but Monica Massie leaned over politely in an attempt to see the twenty-eight-foot inboard-outboard hidden behind the looming stern of the yacht. "Well, isn't that just the cutest thing, honey," she murmured. A silent explosion of laughter burst inside March as she thought of what her father's response would have been to hearing the *Flower* described as cute.

"Monica, look there," Caitlin said suddenly, speaking across March as though she were not present. "Right at the end of the dock. Isn't that. . ."

March looked too, even though no one had asked her to, and saw Simon Wade deep in conversation with Tommy Monday. Tommy in his frayed cutoffs, was gesturing out toward open water, explaining and describing, obviously. Simon was listening intently, nodding and now and then pointing or, it appeared, questioning. A pervasive warmth swept over March, as, without meaning to, she gave a quick downward look at her well-splashed boat shoes and grubby work clothes.

Monica said wonderingly, "Why, for heaven's sake! Isn't that Simon Wade from Palm Beach? What in the *world* do you suppose he's doing in a place like this? Well, Caty honey, it looks as if you're going to have a better time here than you thought."

"It does at that, doesn't it?" Caitlin said, and her tone was no longer bored, Monica noticed. She walked along the dock with a graceful, long-legged stride, her body moving with a kind of deliberate sensual slowness. Monica followed after her eagerly but with less grace, and March watched as they greeted Simon. She could see the surprise in his face, and then he gave Caitlin a quick hug and put out a hand to Monica. Caitlin was animated and laughing now. She turned to point toward the *Ayes of Texas* as though in explanation and March quickly slid back onto her own boat and ducked into the cabin out of sight. When she emerged moments later Simon and the two women were walking away from the marina, up the path toward the hotel. Once she saw him throw back his dark head and laugh. The sound reached her distantly, and March felt her cheeks burn. *What had Caitlin Massie said to make him laugh? And why do I even care?* She turned back to the job of cleaning the *Flower of the Sea,* taking up a clean dry cloth and beginning to work the special wood preserver carefully into the teak trim. Hers was a utility boat, designed for efficiency in the water rather than for showy style and therefore the teak had been kept to a minimum. In forty-five minutes she was finished with her job, the boat so clean and polished that she could think of nothing else to do. She glanced at her watch, remembered that she had promised to meet Paulie for lunch and realized that indeed she was suddenly ravenously hungry. She put away the few remaining things lying about on the deck and carefully locked the small cabin. Then she stepped up onto the dock and started toward shore and the inn.

It was a beautiful Bahamian day. The sun beat down strongly as it always did in the middle of the day but the cooling breeze that blew in early spring made the air fresh and pleasant. March had seen more than one tourist fooled by it. Failing to realize the strength of the tropical sun, they often came in red as cooked lobsters to try and enjoy an evening meal at the hotel after baking all day on the narrow strip of dazzling white sand at the ocean beach.

At the end of the dock she started up the path to the inn. It was covered with a carpet of needles from the pines that grew all around it. To the right of the path were a few privately-owned bungalows. They were low to the ground, surrounded by palm trees and painted in pastel colors as was the local custom. The pinks, blues, yellows, pale greens, and off-whites blended with both the foliage and the boats in the marina. It seemed to March that no matter where you looked on the island you saw color—the pink, white and rose of oleander, the more vibrant hibiscus, the multi-colored leaves of the croton plant. *I was trying to explain it all to him yesterday*, she thought, *make him see it as I do. How foolish it must have sounded to him. He was seeing it all from a different point of view—profit and loss. Investment. I wanted him to feel about it as I do. I'm not a world traveler like him*, she admitted to herself. *The only places I've ever been in twenty-three years—until six months ago—were the trips to Florida with the captain to outfit or repair the boat. But I know—I just know that there's no place on earth more beautiful than that island. And I wanted Simon Wade to see it all through my eyes, to love it as I do. What a perfect fool he must have thought me*, she scolded herself, and tears came into her eyes again, whether from shame or some other emotion she could not tell. *And why am I always crying lately? I never cried in my whole life and now suddenly I seem to do nothing else.*

At the door of the inn she hesitated for a moment, looking down at herself. *I do look awful*, she thought, *but if I go home to change I'll keep Paulie waiting. And anyway, nobody cares at noon. People don't change until the dinner hour.* She pushed the door open abruptly and crossed the lobby. It felt cool inside, and it was dim from the many trees that shaded the building and overhung the veranda. Halfway across the lobby a figure loomed, then approached her, and a familiar voice said, "Well, if it isn't the lady captain. We meet again, March Raffin." There was a bantering note in his voice. March looked up quickly. Her eyes were not quite adjusted to the dimness, but she was sure there was a twinkle of mockery in his dark ones.

"It's a small island, Mr. Wade," she replied coldly.

"True. But look here—about yesterday. I want you to know that—"

"Please. You don't have to explain anything to me," she replied tartly. "I don't own Whispering Pines Cay. You do. I can't expect you to feel as I do about it. And anyway, it's nothing to me."

"You could have fooled me. That was a really silent trip back yesterday afternoon."

"I was paying attention to my navigating."

"Ah yes. You always do that, don't you, Captain?"

March bridled. "And you don't have to keep calling me that."

"Sorry. Actually I was apologizing for something else, if you'd given me a chance to finish. I'm afraid I came on much too strong."

"There's no need to apologize," March said hastily. The memory of that kiss on the windswept bluff over Solitude Point had been with her every moment since yesterday, but she felt she could not bear to hear him mention it. She knew quite well that it had been a

72

small unimportant interlude to him. If it had meant more to her, she did not want to be reminded of it. Quickly she contradicted herself. *It did not mean more to me*, she told herself firmly. *It meant absolutely nothing*.

"It's just that I thought it would be nice if we were able to get along, be friends," he said.

"I don't think there's any need for that either," March said. "I'll be leaving Coral Cay before long."

Now his expression was one of genuine surprise. He frowned down at her. "Leaving? Surely not for good."

"Yes, for good, Mr. Wade."

"But I thought—I mean, you seem to belong here. The way you spoke about the islands—"

"Yes, well—" She gave a small shrug and then glanced behind him. "I believe your friends are coming."

Monica and Caitlin Massie joined them, and Caitlin's slender hand slid around Simon's arm. Monica said, "Simon that was real sweet of you to take us poor lonesome ladies to lunch. Maybe you can find something else for us to do here while my husband goes fishing."

Simon resumed his mockingly polite manner.

"Have you met these ladies, Miss Raffin? Monica and Caitlin Massie."

"We've met," Caitlin purred. "Our—boats—are docked next to each other."

"Ah, how nice. Friendship among boatmen."

March cast him a cold look and said, "Excuse me, will you? I've put in a hard morning working and I'm late for a lunch date. So nice to see you again." She nodded briefly toward Caitlin and Monica and moved away from them.

Simon Wade smiled and nodded as she moved away, but an odd look had flickered across his face at her mention of a lunch date and she could feel his eyes on her back as she walked in what she hoped was a purposeful way to the dining room.

She went directly to the table in the family alcove where Paulie was waiting for her. Although Miss Emily tolerated them both in her kitchen, they knew it was a more prudent policy to sit in the dining room during the busy time of the day when Miss Emily would be moving around the kitchen with the force of a tropical storm and would not look kindly on intruders underfoot. Paulie was sipping cold pineapple juice.

"Here. I ordered one for you. Drink it while it's still cold," she said. "I was dying for you to get here," she went on, bubbling over with her news. "Those people from the big yacht were here. And who do you think they were lunching with? Your friend Simon Wade."

"He's not my friend," March said, and sipped her juice. The dining room, like the lobby, was cool and dim, for which she was grateful.

"Oh?" Paulie's eyebrows went up. "Well anyway, you should have seen those two."

"I did, just now in the lobby."

"Money," Paulie said in a low voice. "You can tell, can't you? We don't get many like that on Coral Cay."

We've got more than enough of them now though, March thought bitterly.

"They didn't look much alike, I didn't think," Paulie said.

"It's stepmother and stepdaughter."

"Is it really? Then you were introduced."

"Yes."

"Well then. That explains it."

"Explains what?"

"The young one's always had money. The older one's just married into it."

March shook her head and laughed. "Paulie, you are an incurable gossip."

"Not at all! I'm a student of human nature."

"Well, I think you've hit it on the head this time."

"Don't I always?" Paulie said smugly. "Look, I ordered lunch for both of us while I was waiting."

Tiny, the waiter who had been with the hotel almost as long as Miss Emily, came up to the table with two steaming bowls of conch chowder and a loaf of fresh baked bread.

"Welcome home, March," he said, putting the bowl in front of her. "Awful sorry about the captain. Awful sorry."

"Thank you, Tiny. It's real good to be back." If the morning of fresh air and exercise had not put March's mind completely at ease, it had at least given her an appetite, and for several minutes she and Paulie were silent as they ate. When their bowls were empty, Paulie sat back and said tentatively, "What about some more?"

March looked reprovingly at her. "What about that five pounds you're planning to lose?"

"Oh, you're right. You're always right." She glanced up as two men entered the dining room and then she nudged March with her foot under the table. "Those two are from the yacht too," she whispered.

March studied them as tactfully as she could without staring outright. They took the table next to the alcove so she could overhear much of what they said. The older of the two looked to be in his late forties and was a large man. Big hands, big feet, and a booming voice that fit him perfectly. He was wearing white slacks and a navy blue knit shirt. The shirt had embroidered lettering over the pocket but March could not make out what it said. The younger man was in his late twenties or early thirties and had curly light hair. He looked to be just short of six feet tall and was as slim as his companion was bulky. Slim in an attractive way, March thought, wiry and athletic-looking. Only for some reason she could not associate

75

him with outdoor exercise. *A health club*, she thought. *I'm sure he belongs to one*. They both ordered the special drink of the house – the goombay smash—a glamorous concoction of pineapple juice, coconut and various other secret ingredients.

"Tell you what, Ted," the big man boomed, "these women are beyond me. I mean, three weeks we spend in Nassau, I let 'em spend half my money, I figure they'll be ready for a quiet week or two at a place like this. But you know I think they're disappointed?"

"I believe they'll survive it," the younger man said mildly.

"You bet your life. Now it's our turn, Teddy. Just us and the Atlantic ocean and all those fish."

March and Paulie glanced at each other, suppressing giggles. The man named Ted seemed to be listening patiently to the older man. He had the air of a practiced listener about him, but March thought the two probably had little in common. In spite of his fit athletic look, it seemed to March there was a touch of langor about him, a look of that same boredom she had seen in Caitlin Massie. His next words reinforced what she was thinking.

"I'll do my best to keep up with you, Stan. Not sure how good I'll be at it."

"Oh shoot, Teddy, you deserve it. Three weeks in Nassau looking after those little gals of mine—taking 'em around to the night spots—you must be ready for a good day on the ocean with fresh air and man talk. I tell you, I got to make it up to you. It woulda wore me out if I'd had to do it."

"Not at all. It was a pleasure for me," the younger man said. "And I appreciate your bringing me along on this trip. It's been a real taste of Texas hospitality."

"Well, any friend of my little Caty's. . ." the big man said, and let his voice drift off as Tiny brought them their plates and he began to pay attention to his

76

food. March, who had been staring at the tablecloth as she listened, raised her eyes slowly and was startled to see the younger man staring directly at her.

"I think you're right, Stan," he said, still not taking his eyes from her. "The best could be yet to come."

"Oh, you're right about that, Teddy," the big man answered, addressing himself heartily to his food. "We'll get going tomorrow at dawn and head for the north shore of Great Guana Cay. Down at the town they were saying a fellow caught a seventy-eight-inch sailfish out there last week."

March, still feeling the young man's eyes on her, moved uncomfortably and turned to Paulie, but Paulie was already pushing her chair back from the table. "I've got to run, March. Daddy asked me to meet the fishing boat today so Miss Emily can start on tonight's specialty. See you at dinner?"

"Yes, okay—" March said, but she was beginning to feel suddenly unprotected, left alone at the table. She watched Paulie leave and wished she did not have to pass so close to the end of the bar where the two men were sitting in order to leave the dining room. She debated whether she should duck out through the kitchen, then decided she was being ridiculous. Yesterday's experience was making her jump at shadows. Resolutely she got up and began walking toward the lobby.

"Excuse me, miss." Even though she had been half-expecting it, the man's voice made her jump. She stopped and looked toward the table. It was the younger man who had spoken and he was still regarding her in that curious, interested way, only now he had risen from his chair. "Didn't I see you at the marina a little while ago?"

"I was at the marina this morning, so I guess you might have seen me there." She felt guarded and defensive, her whole body taut. What did he want with her anyway? And then in the next moment

77

something inside her gave way and relaxed. Had six months in New York changed her so much? She was home now. This was Coral Cay, where strangers spoke to each other and nobody was on guard with anybody. She managed a smile.

"I'm sorry. I know I'm being awfully rude," the man said, and he smiled back at her, showing white even teeth. "My name is Ted Newburn. This is Stan Massie. We pulled in this morning aboard the *Ayes of Texas* ."

Stan Massie waved a fork at her. "Howdy, little lady. Mighty pleased to make your acquaintance," he boomed, making a small gesture of rising, but then sinking at once back into his chair and going on with his meal.

"I'm March Raffin." Now that she was closer, she could see that the lettering over Stan Massie's pocket did indeed say *Ayes of Texas* in carefully casual script. "I met Mrs. Massie and Caitlin this morning while I was working on my boat. I'm docked next to you."

"You're here on vacation?" Ted asked.

"Oh no. I live here. On Coral Cay. I keep my boat at the marina." Ted Newburn's eyes were still on her. March returned his look levelly.

"Well, say then, if you're a native, you must be familiar with the best fishing spots. Stan and I were just making plans for tomorrow. I'll bet you could give us some good tips."

At the word fishing, Stan Massie came to attention and looked at her again. "Is that a fact? You live here? Well, you sit down, little lady. Can I order you a drink?"

"No thank you." March hesitated for a moment, then accepted the chair Ted was holding out. His outright interest was a bit unsettling, but she had to like Stan Massie, with his booming voice, hearty appetite and open, good-natured face.

"Now, tell me, is the north coast of Great Guana Cay as good as they say for marlin and sails?" Stan asked, leaning toward her.

March had never really approved of game fishing any more than Captain Bobby Raffin had, although in years past the captain had run a fishing boat to augment their modest income. *Even so*, she thought, *I mustn't be rude to hotel guests.* And besides, there was a friendliness about Stan that was hard to resist.

"Well, the north coast of Great Guana slopes gradually out to sea for several hundred yards," she explained. "Then the depth drops suddenly to four hundred feet or more, creating a ledge. Deep water fish like marlin and sails spend most of their time in the four hundred-foot water but come near the ledge to feed on the smaller fish that inhabit the shallower water. Try to hire yourself a boat with a fathometer, a depth finder, so you can determine the exact position of the ledge, and then troll with ballyhoo – it's a bait fish you can buy at the marina—but don't go any faster than ten to twelve miles an hour. Maybe you'll get lucky."

"Well, doggone, little lady!" Stan exclaimed heartily. He was staring at her as though in disbelief. "That sounds like the best fishing advice anyone's ever given me. You know your islands all right. Well! Looks as if tomorrow's shaping up into a good day for us, Teddy."

"I'd say things were shaping up all around," Ted agreed, smiling at her quite openly now. March pushed her chair back.

"I really must be getting along," she said. "It was very nice meeting both of you. Good luck fishing tomorrow. We'll probably be running into each other at the marina."

"Hey now, whoa there a minute," Stan said. "We'll do better than that. The Massie ladies are having a little get-together aboard the boat. No, hold on now, Monica says I'm to call it a yacht. Well, aboard the yacht then—day after tomorrow. Dinner, music, that sort of thing. I'd be mighty honored and pleased if you'd join us and sample some of our Texas hospitality."

March quailed inwardly at the thought of spending an entire evening in the shadow of the glamorous "Massie ladies".

"Oh Mr. Massie, that's very kind of you, but I—"

"Now hold up there," Stan boomed. "If you're fixing to say no, why, I just won't take that for an answer. Why, we're neighbors down there on the dock, and neighbors ought to be neighborly. And call me Stan, why don't you? No need to make me sound like I've got one foot in the grave."

"I second that," Ted said. "We won't take no for an answer."

March smiled from one to the other. "All right then. It sounds as if I'm outvoted. And I accept— with pleasure. Thank you for inviting me."

"See you at the party then," Ted Newburn said, and as she turned to leave the dining room she heard him add softly, "If not before."

CHAPTER 5

THERE WAS ONE JOB FACING HER that March had been
dreading, and the next day she got up determined to
face it squarely. She must sort out her father's
belongings and decide what was to be done with them.
After only two days back home, she had already
begun to feel herself drifting back into the island's
routine, falling under its old spell. But the longer she
put off this unhappy chore, the harder it would be.
She knew she could not keep the captain's things.
From now on she would be traveling light and staying
unencumbered. In a small city apartment she would
have room for only the essentials. She would keep
one or two small mementoes and dispose of the rest. *I
don't need anything to keep his memory alive*, she
told herself. It will stay with me always. Even so, a
small knot of cold formed inside her as she contem-
plated the task.

She fixed her own breakfast in her small kitchen
instead of going to the inn where she would surely be
distracted by Paulie's bright chatter and Miss Emily's
tempting food and where she would be apt to run into

Simon Wade, the last person she wanted to see right now. Then she steeled herself to go into her father's room and make a start.

Once she had experienced the first pang of opening his closet and seeing his clothes hanging there, she began to feel a bit more at ease. It was almost as if he were there with her again, and the warmth of their companionship settled around her as in the old days. The clothes she would simply give away, she decided, exactly as Captain Bobby would have done himself, to anyone who needed them. Fishermen and boatmen, the ones he used to sit and swap stories with at the dock. Only not his hat. She did not think she could bring herself to part with that.

While she worked she put some records on the stereo, some that she and her father had liked especially. He had liked the native rhythms and sounds of the islands, but he had been fond also of the opposite extreme: precisely structured chamber music, Mozart and Vivaldi, Bach and Handel. So March had grown up liking music of every sort, and had added to her father's collection with her own younger music, her favorite popular groups and singers. Disposing of the records would be painful. Perhaps she would give them all to Paulie, along with the stereo. She would give Don Sanders the captain's collection of charts and maps. Some of them were handsome enough to frame and hang in the inn's lobby. Only she would keep aside one for herself— the map that charted the safe route to Whispering Pines Cay, all the reefs marked, the island itself shown and even penciled with the captain's notes for settlement. Here the little inn facing the harbor, here the dock. Small x's denoting cottages, and at the southeast tip, on Solitude Point, another x to indicate the house he had always wanted to build for himself.

March stared at the unrolled map for a long time, spreading it out on the bed and weighing down the

corners with books. Even though she willed herself
not to, she could not help seeing the island as it would
be when Simon Wade had finished developing it.
Developing. What an inaccurate word, March
thought, to describe something like the huge, glossy
Bel-Surf hotel. It made her wince to imagine the
fragile island vegetation destroyed, ripped out to
accommodate a mushrooming commercialism. She
went on sorting.

The telescope—that should surely go to Tommy
Monday, who had cared for the *Flower* so faithfully.
The chess set—Tiny the waiter had been his favorite
chess partner—that would be Tiny's. On the table
beside his bed was his old well-worn Bible with scraps
of paper sticking out of it to mark favorite passages.
March opened to one of them: *O Lord, how manifold
are thy works! In wisdom hast thou made them all: the
earth is full of thy riches, So is this great and wide
sea*. Beside it was the small framed picture of her
mother that had stood there as long as March could
remember. She picked it up and looked at it now as
she had done so often in the past. A serene, heart-
shaped face much like her own looked back at her
with clear direct eyes. March had no memory of her
mother except for the picture. A flood of warmth
suffused her now as she felt a sudden nearness to her.
Thinking of Captain Bobby reunited with her in the
life everlasting brought them both so near that their
presence was an almost palpable one to March. She
put aside the Bible and the small pile of things she was
saving for herself and went on working—sorting,
separating, and in spite of herself, remembering.

She did not know how many hours had gone by
when the knock on the door came, making her give a
small start of surprise. It was a sharp, loud rap,
probably so that it would be heard over the music
from the record player. *Paulie*, she said to herself.
Come to remind me that I've missed lunch. She

hurried through the living room and threw the door open. But it was not Paulie; it was Simon Wade standing there.

"I'm sorry," he said. "I didn't mean to make so much noise. I didn't think you'd hear me over the music."

March was speechless for a moment, feeling—as she often did with him – awkward and unpoised. She was dressed for work in cutoff jeans and a T-shirt, while she saw that he was, as usual, immaculate in beige linen bermuda shorts and a green Izod shirt.

"Mr. Wade! I didn't expect—I mean, was there something—"

"I wanted to see where you live," he said frankly. "I asked at the inn."

"I see." They faced each other in the open doorway but March made no move to invite him in. He stood in a casual attitude, his weight on one leg, his hands resting on his hips in a way she had seen before. His expression was one of curious intensity as he regarded her. He seemed to be trying to read her, to figure her out, as though she were a puzzle that he had to keep working at. *You might as well forget it*, March said silently. *No matter how long you figure, we are never going to know each other any better. His next words gave her a shock.*

"I thought perhaps we might get to know each other a little."

March stared at him. Did he have a gift for mind-reading? But the sense of her father's presence was strong in her after several hours of handling his things. And the captain would never have kept a guest standing on the doorstep. "I'm sorry—you startled me a bit, that's all. Won't you come in, Mr. Wade?"

"Couldn't you call me Simon?" he asked with what sounded like a touch of irritability. She had her back to him, so she merely raised her shoulders in a small shrug as she went to the stereo and turned down the volume.

"Very nice," he said. "Vivaldi, isn't it?"

"Yes—*The Four Seasons*. It was a favorite of my father's."

When she turned back to him she saw that he was standing in the middle of the room looking around, taking in the bookshelves with all their well-worn covers, the record cabinet, the comfortable furniture with its bright covers and throws, the woven-grass rugs.

"I like your house, March Raffin," he said.

It would be nice to believe him, but guessing what sort of homes he was used to, what degree of luxury, she thought it very likely he was only being polite. And for what reason? She said nothing but gave the small shrug once more. She supposed she was acting surly and unfriendly. Well, if so, she really cared very little. Nor did she care what Simon Wade might think. Having failed in his lightning approach on Whispering Pines, very likely he was now taking the subtle tack. And only, she was quite sure, for a momentary diversion. He was obviously a man who enjoyed conquests.

"It's a beautiful day," he went on smoothly. "I thought I'd be seeing you down at the marina."

"I had things to do here," she said. "I told you yesterday that I'd be leaving Coral Cay soon—there's a great deal to take care of first."

"You're planning to sell this house then? I should think you'd find it hard to part with."

"I'm getting rather used to doing hard things," March said bitterly. She regretted it the instant the words were out. The last thing she wanted was to sound as if she were making a bid for sympathy from this man. She veered away from the subject.

"There must have been other people at the marina today. Couldn't you find something to do with them? The Massie ladies, for instance?" She used the phrase mockingly, and he caught it at once.

His mouth quirked in a one-sided grin. "Oh, yes indeed. Only I thought I might coax you out for a few minutes. I'd like to see a little more of Coral Cay. Would you show me around?"

"Oh really, I don't think . . . "

"All I've seen so far is the waterfront—the inn and the marina. I know there's more to it than that with all the interesting paths I see running back into the woods. And I happen to know what a first-rate guide you are."

March gave him a quick resentful look, her clear blue eyes meeting his dark ones for a moment. She did not care for his flippancy. She doubted his sincerity, and more, she disliked everything she knew about him, his ideas, his work, his way with women, which seemed to her proprietary and confident. Still, a short walk did not mean getting involved. And in any case, her time here was limited. Once she was gone she would never see Simon Wade again. Perhaps she should relax a little and take the whole thing more lightly. She managed a faint smile.

"All right," she agreed. "Just a short walk. If you don't mind waiting a minute until I tidy up?"

She left him there looking around the living room while she hurried into her own room and shut the door. For a moment she considered putting on one of the smart outfits Melissa had bought her in New York, but then at once she thought how eager that would look, how anxious to appear at her best before him. Instead, she washed her face and hands, ran a brush through her hair until it shone and applied a touch of lipstick. Then she returned to the living room.

He had stepped into her father's room and was standing there looking around, his hands in his pockets. She had left things piled here and there in stacks, but there was still a look of trim, almost nautical order about the room. He turned to her and said, "Sorry. I didn't mean to pry. Perhaps you didn't want me in here."

86

She made a small gesture with one hand. "It doesn't matter. This was my father's room. I've spent the morning sorting his things."

"That must have been hard, too." He turned around, taking in everything – the charts, the telescope, the windows facing out through the moving pines toward the sea.

"Not as hard as I thought it would be," she said truthfully. "It was like having him with me again."

His look fell on the Bible and picture she had left on a corner of the bed. He picked the Bible up and glanced at it. As he put it down his eyes went to the picture. He made no comment, but looked around once more. "A sailor's quarters," he murmured then. "I would have enjoyed knowing your father."

It could be an act, March thought. Certainly his voice had an odd way of changing from sardonic and supercilious to warm and sincere, all in an instant. And right now it seemed to her—but perhaps she only wanted to believe it—that there was a note of sincerity in his voice. But were ever two men more different than Simon Wade and her father?

"Are we ready?" she said.

He followed her out of the house and down the woods path.

"Won't this take us back to the beach?" he asked.

"Wait and see."

Halfway down, another path intersected, and March pointed and turned left. The slope grew steeper as they struck off at an angle, walking upward and now and then stopping to look back through the openings in the trees toward the clear, vibrant blue of the sea.

"Are we going somewhere special?" he asked at last.

"I thought you were interested in seeing something the tourists usually don't."

"I am, but is it a secret?"

"You'll see soon enough. This is a path the islanders know well. This islander, certainly."

"You come here often?"

"Yes. I always have."

"Sounds very mysterious."

They walked on, still climbing, until the trees parted and a large open field, flat and sun-swept, opened before them. In the center of the field, with pine trees at its back, was a small building, weathered and old but sturdy-looking, a small bell tower pointing heavenward.

"A school?" he asked.

"A church. Paulie Sanders and I, and Tommy Monday too, used to walk here every Sunday. With our families, of course, but the three of us always ran ahead. Sometimes Tommy chased us."

"Is it still in use?" he sounded so incredulous that March bristled.

"Of course. Whyever wouldn't it be?" She walked ahead of him across the grassy clearing and shaded her eyes on both sides with her hands to peer in through a window. He did so, too.

"It never changes," she observed, noting the rows of wooden pews, the simple lectern. "I used to sing in the choir. We sat over there. I learned so many things here, important things. I don't think I realized at the time how important they were." For a moment she closed her eyes and it seemed as if she could hear, like the sound from a seashell held to the ear, the strains of an old hymn. *When the roll is called up yonder. . .*

She took a step back and found Simon Wade looking at her. For a moment March felt a sensation of unsteadiness, almost of dizziness. The day was warmer than she had thought, the air heavy and sultry. Everything around them was still—the trees, the tall grasses, the air itself. Nothing stirred.

"And what did you get out of all that?" he asked, studying her.

"A faith to live by, to sustain me, to comfort me, to give meaning to my life. Acceptance of Christ has given me all that. I wouldn't expect my boat to ride out a storm without an anchor, now would I? Well—" She nodded toward the little church. "This is my anchor. It holds me fast, even during the roughest times."

"I keep learning about you," he murmured.

March swallowed and tried to hold onto her composure. "I think that's the whole picture," she whispered. "Nothing more to know."

His eyes were holding her with their deep direct stare.

"I think there must be much more." Very slowly his hand reached out to touch her hair. His touch made March tremble and she felt a warmth all over that was quite separate from the heat of the day. At the same moment a cloud moved over the sun and the air seemed suddenly more oppressive than ever.

"We'll have a storm later," she said in a low voice.

"Do you really think so?" He was still studying her.

The feeling of confusion was still jumbling March's thoughts, sending them out in all directions, helter-skelter. *What are we talking about?* she thought wildly. *The weather or something entirely different?* He moved slightly so that he was standing closer to her.

She stepped away from him and said hastily, "Do you know what that is?" She pointed toward a shelf by the church door. It was a small one and had been put within easy reach of the door. A huge conch shell rested on it. It looked satiny as though from much handling and it gleamed in pale shades of pink and white. She stole a look at him. His expression had turned cool and impersonal once again, the uptilted eyes slightly mocking.

"No—"

"It's the Sunday school bell," she said. "Or the island equivalent. Our teacher used to blow on that to call us to our class. The regular bell was saved for the grownups' church service."

"You're kidding!" There was real astonishment in his voice.

"You're in the islands now, Mr. Wade," she said, feeling her composure returning to her and feeling, too, another touch of indignation at his surprise. "We're a little backward by your standards, I imagine, but some of us like it that way."

Without saying any more, she turned and headed back across the clearing toward the path. Suddenly she felt the need to get away from the nearness of his strong masculine presence, the touch of his hand on her hair, above all from the emotional response he seemed to generate in her. She could hear him following after her, but neither of them spoke for a time while they threaded their way down through the woods to the place where the two paths intersected. March paused there and Simon said in a puzzled way, "Look, did I say something wrong up there?"

In spite of herself March smiled. "No, of course not. I'm afraid I was being a little defensive. I thought perhaps you were thinking that we're pretty primitive here." It was only part of the truth but it was as much as she was willing to express aloud.

He said, "Do you mind not doing my thinking for me?" He smiled as he said it, but she thought that a note of cold seriousness lay behind the smile.

"Sorry," she said, thinking to herself, *will we ever be able to talk together sanely, without animosity?*

He, too, seemed to want to get the conversation back to a pleasanter level. "Look, there's still a bit of the afternoon left, and the sun's back. Shall we get our suits and go for a swim?"

"A swim?"

"Why not?"

"Well, I don't know . . . "

"Maybe out on that reef to the right of the marina? There should be tropical fish there. They can stare at us and we'll stare back."

"If you want to go to the reef and see things—I mean, the fish and the coral and all that—you really should go with snorkeling equipment. That's the best way."

"Wonderful! Where can we get it?"

March did not answer for a moment and then she said hesitantly, "Well, I have it at the house."

Exactly what I told myself I was not going to do, March thought despairingly as the two of them made their way in the *Flower of the Sea* toward the reef that stood offshore from the marina. The one thing she had promised herself to avoid was any involvement with Simon Wade, and here she was spending a whole afternoon with him, showing him the sights and probably appearing to him as vulnerable as any schoolgirl. He was sure to take it as a sign of interest on her part. Her old argument returned and she grabbed for it, almost too quickly. Her time on the island was limited. What harm could this small interlude do when she would soon be gone for good and both the island and Simon Wade would be part of the past?

"This will do, I think," she said, cutting the engine. "Ready with the anchor?"

'Aye aye, Captain," he grinned and went quickly forward to cast it off the bow. In his swimming trunks he looked more than ever lithe and muscular. He moved effortlessly and with smooth coordination. Without meaning to, March felt an almost uncontrollable impulse to reach out and touch the smooth rippling skin of his arms and the chest that were lightly covered with fine dark hair.

"Will you burn?" he asked, standing beside her once more, and March gave a start of surprise, since she was feeling a pervasive inner heat from her thoughts.

"I don't know—that is, I suppose I might." She was wearing a T-shirt over her bathing suit.

"I only wondered, because if you've spent a whole winter in New York you might be sensitive."

"Well, yes, I suppose I might," March said, feeling flustered and confused.

"Have to be cautious the first time out."

"Yes, you're right. I should have brought sunscreen."

"I stuck a bottle of it in my pocket. Here. Help yourself." He held it out to her. Awkwardly, feeling his look, she lifted off her shirt and began smoothing the lotion over her arms and legs, her neck and shoulders. He said nothing, merely stood a little apart in that loose, relaxed way of his. The blue bathing suit she had not worn in months had never seemed skimpy to her before, March thought furiously. She began to wish he would say something. His silence created a thick tension between them that seemed almost a tangible thing. Added to the oppressive heat it gave March a stifled feeling. She would almost have preferred him to make a remark so that she could come back with a tart answer. But all he said, at long last was, "I don't believe you can reach your back."

She stood quite still for an instant, the plastic bottle in her hand, and then hesitantly, she handed it to him and turned around. Slowly and methodically he began to apply the sunscreen lotion to her back, beginning at the center, between her shoulder blades, and working outward and down. The circling strokes were firm yet gentle. In spite of the tropical sun that was glancing off the water diamond-bright, March felt a shiver run through her. His hand hesitated for a fraction of a second and she knew he had noticed the shiver. But he said nothing and went on applying the lotion. When he finished he said, "There. That ought to protect you."

"Thank you," March whispered. But inside her thoughts raced madly and she felt the increased tempo of her heart. I need more protection than that, she thought anxiously. And a small inner voice seemed to answer her. Against him? Or against yourself? She knew well enough that physical attraction was a long way from being love. Dangerous shoals, she thought.

They laughed at each other's appearance as they put on the equipment.

"You know how it works?" March asked.

"I've done it a few times. Not here, but in Corfu, off Greece. I suppose it's the same."

"Yes, of course. What about gloves? I have them, but if you're not collecting specimens you really don't need them."

"I don't care about collecting," he said. "I'm just planning on looking." She was still aware of his nearness, but this time she ignored it with an effort.

"Well then, I guess we're ready," she said, adjusting her mask and slipping over the side. He followed, swimming beside her with long easy strokes, adjusting his pace to hers. *I will remember this always*, March thought as they swam side by side along the surface, propelled by their flippers toward the coral reef that skimmed close to the surface and caused the water to riffle over it. They swam with their heads down, looking through their masks and breathing through the snorkels, the narrow tubes sticking up above the water. She could see the movement of the water that he made at her side and follow the long pull of each stroke of his arms. They were swimming in thirty feet of water, crystal-clear all the way to the bottom. As they approached the reef it grew shallower, its sandy bottom seeming only an arm's length away, the great branched formations of coral looming about them like exotic trees. They were breathing easily with the snorkels still above the water, but presently March took a deep breath and dived. The sandy bottom, which had looked so near, was actually ten feet down, but she reached it swiftly and with her hand reached out to stir up the white wand of the bottom. Instantly a horde of small tropical fish swarmed around them. They were of every imaginable shade and hue— green, red, pink, blue, shimmering silver, palest gold, yellow. Some were irridescent and seemed to combine every color in one small body. Others were striped, banded, spotted. Although she had surprised them they did not scatter in fright, but after their first surge, began swimming around them. March could see Simon, who had followed her down, looking around in wonder at them, watching them swim past him, pivot, turn, rush past him again in the opposite direction. He put out a hand and a swarm of tiny pink fish swept by it, brushing against it as they went. March could not see his expression behind his mask but she knew somehow that it all delighted him. She gave a kick that sent her to the surface where she blew sharply through the air tube to clear it of water and then dived again. Once more he followed her lead.

She lost track of time when as they dived and rose, swam and circled among the coral, following the tiny fish and then turning about to find themselves followed, as if it were a game of underwater tag. It was a strange other-worldly place of grace and enchantment, of color and fantasy, of movement and deep stillness. Once March saw him linger, quite motionless, as a small flat fish, violet with black stripes, paused only inches from his mask, the two of them staring at each other for a long moment before the fish darted away. Once when he reached out to touch a branch of red fire coral, March thrust herself over to his side and seized his arm, motioning a warning with her free hand, signaling danger wordlessly, unable to explain at the moment that it would cause a burning sensation. He turned to her in surprise and put his own hand over hers on his arm and for a second or two held her so, before she gave a sharp kick and rose to the surface for another breath.

At last she signaled to him that she was tired and wanted to rest, but with one hand she motioned him back, letting him know he could continue diving as long as he cared to. She swam lazily back to the boat, took off her mask, mouthpiece and flippers and tossed them into the boat, then clung idly to the ladder at the stern of the boat and watched as he made a few more dives and then swam toward her The sun shone glistening on his muscular, wet arms with every stroke as he raised them out of the water. *I will remember this afternoon always*, March thought. *I will save it. It will go back to New York with me along with the few memories I can pack in my suitcase. And that's all it will be, a memory.*

He dived under the surface and disappeared for a few moments only to pop up right beside her. He removed his mask and flippers as she had. March guessed that even though his feelings might not be the same as hers he had enjoyed the experience, for he said at once, "We don't have to go right back, do we?"

"Soon, I'm afraid."

"One short swim then. Without the equipment."

"All right."

They swam around the boat in opposite directions, laughed when they met each other, and returned to the ladder astern, clinging to it wearily.

"That was wonderful," he said, looking at her. "It's beautiful out there on the reef." His dark hair glistened with wetness, and water dripped off his tanned shoulders. March pushed her own hair back.

"You seem to get along well with our Bahamian fish. I saw one that was quite taken with you."

He gave her a look that was curiously tender. "You're a little bright fish yourself, March, quick and graceful. And beautiful."

95

The warning voice deep inside March tried to break through. Don't be fooled, don't be gullible, it whispered, but for once March did not listen. It can't matter, can it? she asked this more sensible self. Does it really matter, just for this one afternoon? And then there was no chance for further thought, for his arm came around her, pulling her against him, and his lips were on hers in a kiss that carried with it a taste of sea and sun, and that sent flames like the touch of fire coral along all her nerves and muscles. He held her close against him and she felt the push of water around them. The noise of the surf was in her ears, rising to a crescendo until March could not tell which was the sea and which was her heart pounding. She was no longer holding to the ladder. Her arms had come up to circle his neck. His strength held her up.

Even though March was not thinking clearly, she knew that this kiss was different from the kiss on Whispering Pines Cay. There was a more insistent passsion in him now, a deeper response in her. And suddenly the small inner voice made itself heard with that one word—danger. Too much, too soon, it murmured. Time to stop, to think, to remember what matters, what values you want to hold fast to. The senses could be persuasive, March knew. They could betray you. Lust was not love, no matter how it might seem in an unguarded moment. She had associated danger with Simon Wade before this. Today she had not wanted to think such thoughts. But had anything changed? She pulled away.

"It's getting late," she said. "We really should be starting back."

He looked at her long and hard, studying her face, and there seemed to be a questioning there, as though there were things he would like to ask her. But he did not.

"Yes, all right," he said in a flat expressionless voice. And then he added, "But thank you for this afternoon."

She scrambled up the ladder, dried herself quickly with a towel and then slipped into her shirt. "If you wouldn't mind getting the anchor—" she said.

"Aye aye, Captain," he answered, and his tone was once more that half-mocking, half amused one. The moment that had pulled them close together, clinging and seeking each other wildly, had evaporated. He glanced, squinting, at the bright sky. "I think you were wrong about that storm coming," he said.

She turned away and gave her attention to starting up and heading the boat toward the distant marina. She did not answer him, but to herself she thought, *I'm not so sure.*

Back at the dock he helped her make the boat fast in its slip, helped her pull on the canvas cover, then climbed lightly to the dock and turned to offer her a hand, but she had already followed him up without his aid.

There was a small rustling movement from the slip next to them where the *Ayes of Texas,* massive and luxurious, moved gently at its mooring. Caitlin Massie, who must have been lying on deck sunning, rose and stepped down onto the dock. She was wearing the briefest of white bikinis and she looked long-legged and golden in the late afternoon sun, her silky hair loose around her shoulders. Her soft southern drawl addressed them lazily.

"Well! You two have been putting in an afternoon of it, haven't you? I *thought* I saw you out on that reef."

"Hello, Caitlin," Simon said. "Your dad back from fishing?"

"We're just waiting for him." March guessed that the waiting was not occupying all of Caitlin's thoughts. "Simon, we're expecting you to dinner on board tonight, you know."

"Oh yes. I'd forgotten." He glanced toward March.

"Do excuse me, won't you?" March said hastily. "I must get home. I have a million things to do."

She did not look at Simon's face again, but she glanced at Caitlin's just before she turned and left, and the look she saw there was one of pure hatred.

CHAPTER 6

SHEER LUXURY!" Paulie exclaimed, kicking off her sandals and putting her feet up on March's couch. March sat opposite her in a chair and her feet, too, were bare. Between them on a low table was a plate of Miss Emily's special sandwiches, all the fillings succulent, all the crusts removed. Beside it stood a pitcher of iced tea and two glasses. March had been more than glad to see Paulie when she answered the knock at the door and found her standing on the doorstep bearing the plate of mounded sandwiches. Paulie's face, pink-cheeked and guileless, was a refreshing lift to her spirits.

"Oh, Paulie, what a wonderful idea!" she had exclaimed. "I'm so glad you came."

Paulie, eyebrows raised, had observed mildly, "Well! I didn't know it was going to make that much of a hit." And, after she had come inside, "I just had to get away—haven't sat down all day. But no complaints. It looks like the start of a good season. Only between answering questions at the desk and putting people in the right rooms, tearing around with extra towels—I'm exhausted!"

March had hurried to make a pitcher of tea and the two of them had sat across from each other, lazily and companionably, as they had on a thousand other evenings. Only now, looking at March's faraway expression, Paulie said, "I suppose a penny's not enough to offer for thoughts these days."

March came to attention. "Oh. Sorry. I was just thinking about tomorrow night."

"The party? On board the Massies' yacht?"

"I wish I hadn't said I'd go."

"March, you've got to be kidding!"

"I don't know why I ever let Mr. Massie talk me into it."

"But it'll be fun. Tommy heard that some people are coming from Grand Bahama—you know, people with yachts at Freeport—"

"But I don't belong in that world, Paulie, not at all." It was this feeling of not belonging that had been on her mind ever since she had left Simon at the dock with Caitlin earlier. The only times she had ever felt at ease with him had been when they were off by themselves, away from any contact with the real world. The day on Whispering Pines when they had hiked and laughed and talked—at least until the moment when he kissed her and broke the carefree mood. Today on the reef, diving and swimming in an underwater fantasy world. She had been able to feel free and to enjoy herself with him then. But when reality and the present intruded—she thought of the malice distorting Caitlin's beautiful face—then the illusion was shattered. And that's all it was, an illusion, she told herself. She was already dreading the party, knowing he was sure to be there.

"Would it matter if I just didn't go? I'd never be missed."

Paulie's face softened with understanding. "But you're so pretty, March. There won't be anybody there with your looks."

"Oh Paulie, you're just loyal. But that's ridiculous."

"And besides, you had a good enough time today," Paulie teased. "I saw you out there on the reef with Simon Wade. And having yourself a wonderful afternoon. Now don't deny it."

"Yes, that's true, it was fun, only. . . ." March hesitated, not knowing how to explain what she was feeling to practical Paulie, to whom things were always plain and open, all corners squared and her own sunny disposition lighting every dark recess.

"That Caitlin Massie has quite a temper, I think," Paulie chattered on. "I was on the veranda fixing old Mrs. Halliwell's reclining chair when you went out on the boat, and I could see her watching you just after you left the dock. Of course you were too far away for anyone to see you very clearly once you got to the reef. She would have got out the binoculars to watch, I'm positive, only I suppose she was afraid someone might catch her at it." March, remembering the kisses as the two of them clung to the boat, was relieved that they had been protected by distance.

"But mad?" Paulie went on with a grin. "You should have seen her—it really stuck out all over. Her stepmother went and hid, I think. Then later Mrs. M. and that Ted Newburn fellow who travels with them—an unpaid escort is my guess—they hired a small boat to go off to another island, shopping or sightseeing, I guess. Only Miss Caitlin, her nibs, wouldn't budge. She stayed right on the battlements."

"She was there when we got back," March admitted. "To remind him he was invited to dinner on the boat."

"Aha. That's where he is now?"

"Yes, and she's welcome to him," March said with sudden bitterness, thinking of him aboard the Massie's yacht with golden Caitlin.

"You got a touch of burn today, do you know that?" Paulie said with a meaningful look.

"What?"

"Sunburn. Just a touch."

"Oh." March hugged herself, holding both her bare arms above the elbows and feeling the warmth of her skin. "Well, maybe a little. I used sunscreen though." And at the memory of Simon Wade's hands smoothing the lotion on her bare back, those long strokes that were like caresses, she suddenly jumped up from her chair and crossed the room so that her back was to Paulie.

"Well, if you decide not to go to the party you can always come moonlight swimming with Tommy and me. Only I think you'd be crazy to."

March turned back to her. Once it had been the three of them on every outing—fishing, snorkeling, boating, picnicking on the beach. Now it had such a wistful sound, an echo of times that would not come again. No matter how much she longed for it, March sensed that there would be no return to such simple pleasures. Feeling a lump in her throat, she changed the subject abruptly.

"I started cleaning things out here today," she said. "Dad's things mostly. But there's other stuff I'll have to find a place for."

"But you haven't sold your house yet. What's the rush?"

"Just thinking ahead. When I do sell it I'll pack the books in cartons; you can have them. And the records and the player—I'll give those to you, too."

"I won't take them," Paulie said flatly.

March frowned. "What do you mean?"

"I mean, not as a gift, not to keep. I'll take care of them for you, that's all. When the time comes that you want them again they'll be there for you."

"Oh, Paulie—"

"Now don't go all sad again. It's a simple fact, that's all. Things won't always be this way, March. You think they will, but they won't. I'll take good care of anything you want to leave with me, but it'll still be yours. Understood?"

March nodded helplessly. "All right. Understood."

Last thing at night, after Paulie had gone and before she got into bed, March looked out of the window in her father's room, which had the best view down toward the sea. Through the pines that were bending and swaying in the night wind she could see, twinkling mistily at the dock, the lights of the *Ayes of Texas*, and it almost seemed that she could hear faint laughter drifting out from it. It was later, sometime during the night, when the thunderstorm woke her. She thought in sleepy confusion, *I knew a storm was coming. I said so, didn't I?*

Next morning she had still not decided about the party, but she was determined to stay away from the inn, the beach, the dock, from anyplace where she might encounter Simon Wade. She felt a need to be by herself, to make decisions, to set her thoughts in order. She had been drifting these last two days, allowing herself to be carried this way and that on the current of her emotions. And the only place it had taken her had been into hazardous territory. Time to back off, think things through, get back on course. First of all she would write a letter to Melissa, something she had been putting off too long.

She put a record on the player, turned it down so that the music was only a soft background and sat down at her small desk in the living room to compose her letter. The phrases came to her pen readily even though she knew them to be hollow and without any real substance. *Everyone has been so nice to me. They all seem happy I'm back. Of course I started at once getting things sorted out, and Don Sanders thinks I will have very little trouble selling either the house or the boat. I want to thank you and Bill so much for your great kindness to me and to Dad.*

The soft music wove in and out of her thoughts. She

had put on one of her favorite records by Gina Leigh. She was an artist whose singing had always moved March strongly with its sultry tones, with its tender mourning for lost love. She was glad Paulie had refused to take the records as an outright gift. Maybe sometime, somewhere, she would be able to enjoy them again, she thought wistfully.

She gave an uneasy start when the knock on the door came, and as she got up to answer it, began making hasty resolves in her head. *If it should* be Simon Wade, I'll be casual. If he asks me about the party on the yacht I'll say I may not be able to make it. If he says anything about last night I'll just act off handed—it's nothing to me after all.

But it was Caitlin Massie and Ted Newburn standing on her doorstep. Caitlin was wearing white shorts and a red blouse. A casual outfit, March thought, except for the fact that nothing she put on ever looked really casual. She wore everything with such an air. Always had money, Paulie had said, and it showed. Ted was in white slacks and a yellow knit shirt, looking well and expensively dressed as he always did. An unpaid escort, Paulie had said, and March thought that Paulie, with her simple directness, had sketched in the two of them correctly.

"Hi," Caitlin said. There was no trace now of the resentment March had seen in her face the previous afternoon. She seemed to be making a stab at civility—almost friendliness. Ted Newburn looked at ease; March suspected nothing ever upset him for long.

"Good morning," she said, and Ted put in quickly, "Forgive us for dropping in on you this way, March. It's just that your island is a bit short of telephones."

"It's all right. Come in," March said, and held the door open wide for them. "I was just listening to music and writing letters."

"What a darling house," Caitlin said warmly,

turning around in the middle of the room, and March, remembering her expression at their last meeting, guessed that Caitlin could turn on the charm whenever the need arose. Only what need was motivating her now? *Perhaps after last night she feels I'm not competition any more.*

"Well, if you've forgiven us for bursting in on you," Ted said, "the fact is that we have a small favor to ask."

It had to be, March thought. Caitlin Massie would never come calling out of pure friendliness. "Is there something I can do?" she asked hesitantly, looking from one to the other.

"Daddy told me he's invited you to our little party tonight," Caitlin said. "I'm so pleased. But the local musicians have to leave early to play somewhere else. They were already booked, unfortunately. So we'll have no music after ten, and we simply can't keep the party going without music."

"So we inquired at the hotel about records," Ted put in. "And the young lady there told us . . . "

"Pauline Sanders?"

"Yes, Pauline. She told us you have the best collection of records locally."

"And that you might come to our rescue and lend us some for the evening," Caitlin said. "We brought very few with us, unfortunately."

"Of course," March said. "Please take whatever you want. Look through that bottom shelf, won't you? Most of what you want would be there." She did not mind lending the records. She was, mentally, already packing them away, placing them in her past. Only it did make her feel cornered, since they were obviously assuming she would be coming to the party. Some of this uncertainty must have shown in her face, for as Caitlin moved away to look at the album covers, Ted said, "You are coming, aren't you?" March thought that in spite of his outwardly superficial air, there was a degree of discernment about Ted that he kept hidden most of the time.

"I'm not sure," she said. "I've been rather busy."

"Oh, but you must come," he said with a disarming smile. "We're counting on you. And Stan would be quite upset if you didn't. I suspect he'll have a fish story a mile long to tell you."

March hesitated for a moment longer, then smiled. "All right," she agreed. "Of course I'll come."

"Oh, but you have a marvelous collection!" Caitlin exclaimed brightly, picking out records at random— show tunes and popular groups. "And that one you have on right now—Gina Leigh, isn't it?"

"Yes."

"Oh, that's lovely. Isn't it, Ted? We must have that one. That is, may we?" she said sweetly to March.

March hesitated once more, but only for an instant, then replied, "Yes, of course. It's a particular favorite of mine."

"We'll treat it *very* carefully," Caitlin promised as March took the record from the player and slipped it into its cover to hand to her.

"You might want some of these over here," March said. "They're native island music."

"Oh, yes, by all means. That would be very nice."

Caitlin turned, cradling a dozen albums in the crook of her arm. "Well, we must run and let you get back to your letter-writing. Here, Teddy, you'd better take half. I don't want to drop anything."

She reached out to hand Ted some of the records, and March thought he moved hesitantly, almost with reluctance, to take them. He seemed suddenly uncomfortable, ill at ease. Caitlin, appearing blandly unaware of any change, made her way to the door.

"Thanks again, March. See you tonight!" she called out cheerily, and Ted followed her, murmuring a goodbye but not turning to March again.

March closed the door on them, faintly puzzled, but

putting Ted's attitude down to something that had previously passed between them. She dismissed it from her mind, thinking instead of her own promise to attend the party. *No getting out of it now*, she thought ruefully. *I'll have to go. But I'll just put in an appearance and let Stan Massie tell me his fish story, then I'll duck out. I'll never be missed, I'm sure of that. And if I'm lucky maybe I'll be able to avoid Simon Wade altogether.* But even with her resolution, she found her thoughts in a state of turmoil when she tried to return to the letter she had been writing, and it took all her powers of concentration to finish it off decently. When it was sealed and stamped she walked down the path to the inn to leave it with the day's outgoing mail. It was another fine day after the night's rain, all the trees and blossoms looking moist and refreshed.

Paulie caught up with her on the veranda as she was hurrying to return home.

"Did you decide? About tonight?"

"I guess I'm stuck with it," March said, and told her about the loan of the records.

"You didn't mind, did you? That I sent them to you? I did tell them about the record shop in Johnsville, only Caitlin said they wouldn't have time to get over there today."

"No, of course I didn't mind."

"Then if you're going, for goodness sake come and dress here in my room. You don't want to go staggering down that path of yours in heels."

"I hadn't thought—" March began. I mean, I won't be dressing up that much."

"Well, come anyway," Paulie ordered. "I have to run now, but don't forget."

"All right." March waved and turned away as Paulie banged back through the screen door into the inn. Before she could leave the porch, however, she was stopped by the sound of a familiar voice and she paused. It seemed to be a telephone conversation from the inn lobby, where one of Coral Cay's few telephones was located.

"Slow. Very slow," Simon Wade's voice was saying. "I've been in touch with them every day but it's hard to pin them down. Well, you know what government offices are." There was a pause. "No, I have no doubts about it. They were receptive, but they move slowly. We'll go ahead with our plans as scheduled. Be ready to move as soon as we get the approval." Another pause. "Yes. Getting the heavy equipment in there, that's got to be managed carefully. If the government won't install adequate markers we'll have to do it ourselves—buoys, lights and so on. Too risky the way it is—nothing but a pole and a rag to show the reefs." And after a moment, "What about the generator? Did you find . . . good, that sounds all right. Because of course we'll have to have power we can depend on . . . oh, sure, I've looked it over carefully. Terrific. Couldn't be better . . . "

March hurried off the porch and walked home quickly, anger rising from deep inside her at every step as she realized that all the day before she had allowed herself to forget what Simon Wade was doing here at the islands, and what he was planning to do to Whispering Pines Cay. *I won't forget it again though*, she thought grimly. *And I'm not going to delay any longer putting the house and boat up for sale. I'll talk to Don Sanders about it and see what steps to take. There's no point in putting it off. The sooner I get back to New York and start making a new life, the better off I'll be.*

She arrived back at her house full of resolve to continue her packing and sorting, but there was a restlessness in her and she found it hard to settle down to the job. In the shed behind the house where firewood and tools were kept she found her bike looking as clean and shiny as the boat, and she guessed that it, too, must have received Tommy's attention. On an impulse she decided to go for a ride by herself. She felt a sudden urge to put all obligations, worries, plans for the future, most of all, all thoughts of Simon Wade, completely away from her for the afternoon.

She pedaled down the path from her house and then on past the inn and marina. She passed a stand selling woven bags and baskets, a cluster of small houses belonging to native Bahamians—some of them of them employed by the inn—out onto the narrow causeway road that led from Coral Cay to the larger Coral Island. The sea wind blew her hair back from her face and all her muscles seemed to stretch and relax as she pedaled. She met few cars, but those she did see were driving on the left, which gave March a comfortable feeling of security after six confusing months in New York where every cab she stepped into seemed to her to be driving on the "wrong" side.

In a surprisingly short time she had covered the miles to the town of Johnsville, the island's main settlement, which had a number of hotels that attracted tourists, as well as a busy main street with bright shops and restaurants. The ride had made her hungry, and she stopped at a small restaurant for tea and a sandwich. When she came out and started to get back on her bike, she was stopped by the sight of two familiar figures strolling down the opposite side of the street. Ted Newburn and Caitlin. They appeared to be on a leisurely outing, pausing now and then to peer into shop windows. March had no desire to see them again. She got on her bike and turned back the way she had come before they could notice her. But as she rode back she kept remembering what Caitlin had told Paulie—that they would have no time to shop for records before the party. Of course plans were apt to change, March pointed out to herself, trying to be fair. Yet she could not rid herself of the feeling that Caitlin had come to her house that morning for a reason more devious than mere borrowing. March gave herself a little shake as though to clear away cobwebby thoughts, and scolded herself for inventing stories again. All well and good to do it when it involved only strangers whom you'll never see again, March Raffin, she said sternly. But this is getting close to home, and it's not good. Stick to facts and stay out of trouble. She picked up speed, pedaling faster and hearing the wind sing in her ears as she flew along.

"What do you think?" she asked Paulie. She stood in front of the mirror in Paulie's room at the hotel and turned this way and that in front of the mirror. Paulie's room was much like the girl herself—cosy, friendly, a bit disheveled. Sandals stuck out from under the bed where Paulie had slipped out of them. Magazines lay in an untidy pile in one corner. Paulie herself sat in jeans and a T-shirt in the middle of the bed, knees out sideways, bare feet together in front of her. Her orange cat, Marcus, snoozed on one corner of the bed, opening an eye now and then to keep track of events.

Paulie regarded March critically. "You always look terrific, March. Only do you think it's quite, you know, grand enough?"

March looked again at the pale pink blouse and deeper rose skirt. "It's grand enough," she said firmly. "With my white sandals—" She slipped into them, and the high-heeled sandals with their tiny criss-cross straps did give the outfit a dressier look.

"But what about the other dress you brought?"

"I think this will do very well."

"Well, let me just *see* it," Paulie begged.

Reluctantly March reopened the small overnight case she had brought with her and brought out the white dress she had found when she unpacked.

"I think it's too—" she began, but Paulie ordered, "Try it on, for goodness sake!"

110

March took off the blouse and skirt and slipped the white dress over her head. Slim and soft, it fell to the floor. She faced Paulie apprehensively.

"Oh, March!" Paulie had been holding her breath. Now she let it out in a long sigh. "That's just—you look beautiful! You must wear that."

March looked at her reflection and saw a stranger looking back at her—a taller, elegant, more sophisticated stranger, every curve of her slender body shaped by the caressing fabric, one sun-tanned shoulder bare. *He's never seen me really dressed up. 8ro The thought leaped into her head before she could stop it.*

"Are you sure it's all right?" she asked uncertainly.

"It's stunning! Perfect," Paulie insisted. "Now come on. You're late already."

"It's terribly plain, isn't it?" March asked, still hesitating. "I mean—bare? I haven't any jewelry to wear."

There was a knock at the door, and in answer to Paulie's call, it opened softly. Miss Emily stood there, regal in her white apron and red scarf. "Just wanted to see—" she began, and then as her eyes went to March, "March! Honey, is that really you?"

"Is it all right, do you think, Miss Emily?" March asked anxiously, knowing Miss Emily would be completely honest.

"Perfect. Only need one little thing," Miss Emily said. "And it's just what I was bringing you." She crossed to where March stood at the mirror and held out a single white hibiscus blossom. "Belongs right here," she said, and tucked it into March's hair, which tonight had been pulled back in a French twist. March hesitated, looking at the flower just behind her ear and at Miss Emily's reflection behind her own. The woman said softly, as if she had been reading March's thoughts, "Jewelry's for the ones who need it, honey."

111

"Yes, oh, that's perfect!" Paulie cried, pressing her two palms together. "March, you're going to have a wonderful time tonight!"

March managed a small smile for her friend in the mirror, but inside she could feel a small fist of anxiety forming. *Maybe*, she was thinking.

"I got to hurry back," Miss Emily said, retreating hastily. "Kitchen's every which way. You have a grand time now, you hear?"

"Thank you, Miss Emily," March called after her. As she looked back at the mirror she caught a quick exchange of looks between Paulie and the older woman. It lasted only an instant but it seemed to March there was question on Miss Emily's face and that it was answered by a small barely perceptible shake of the head from Paulie. Miss Emily let herself out and closed the door, and March turned around. "Is anything wrong?"

Paulie smiled quickly. "Of course not. Except that I think you're going to be treated to one huge fish story from that Mr. Massie. Miss Emily's in an awful snit because he's got a blue marlin as big as Moby Dick in the cooler off the kitchen. Caught it today, so be prepared for a blow-by-blow."

"Good. It'll give me something to do at this party. I'm afraid I'm going to be out of my league." Somehow March did not think the exchange of looks had anything to do with Stan Massie or his fish.

Paulie asked a little diffidently, "March, how much do you like Simon Wade really? I mean, have you fallen in love with him?"

"For heaven's sake, no!" March said with spirit. "The more I know about him the less I like him."

"I just wondered," Paulie said, but March thought she looked relieved. *Why did she ask me that?* March wondered. *And what would her look have been if I'd told her the truth?*

CHAPTER 7

IT WAS DARK BY THE TIME SHE LEFT the hotel. Admiring looks from the whole Sanders family and guests on the veranda of the inn followed her down the walk to the marina. Lights were strung along the dock and twinkled all over the big white yacht at the end of it. The marina was shaped like a huge T, with the wooden walkway extending out and then meeting another dock at right angles. At the very corner formed by the two, March's boat nestled, nose into the dock. The *Ayes of Texas* rode parallel with the dock, snuggled up next to it and tonight, March could see, a small gangplank had been put out for the guests' convenience. Unfamiliar boats belonging to the party-goers dotted the marina.

Music was coming from the boat—sounds of a guitar and soft island voices singing. Conversation and laughter drifted out on the warm evening air. March walked slowly. A couple was ahead of her, well-dressed and affluent-looking. They were laughing and talking together and had not noticed her. March lagged back a little to let them get aboard first. She was feeling a nervous tightening in her stomach and was suddenly overcome with shyness. All around her were the familiar sights she was so used to by day – the marine store where fishing supplies were sold, the gas pumps, the rough table where fish were cleaned. She could hear the lapping of water against the sides of boats, the metallic clink of rigging against masts, the creak of mooring lines as they stretched taut. All the sights, sounds, and smells that she had known her whole life, yet she felt herself walking along them tonight like a stranger. At the foot of the gangplank she hesitated, then took a deep breath and walked up, picking her way carefully in her high heels.

At the top she stepped easily onto the rear deck of the yacht and stood for a moment looking around. The two musicians were sitting there, both of them in white with scarlet cummerbunds, playing guitars and singing a familiar island song. She saw that most of the women were in long bright-colored dresses or pants outfits. The men looked more casual—some were even in shirtsleeves, but the shirts were of silk, March noted. There was a casual elegance even about those who went tieless. She stood there taking it all in for a moment, and although several faces turned her way no one recognized her. Then suddenly a man who had been standing in a group looked up and at once started toward her. She saw that it was Ted, and that his face wore a look of surprise as he realized who she was. He was wearing designer jeans and a light soft jacket in a creamy color. Its sleeves were pushed up toward his elbows and his shirt collar stood up in back. As he made his way across the deck toward her, smiling, there was a movement from the open doorway to the cabin at March's left, and Simon came on deck. He stood there for only a second, just long enough for March to take in the white silk shirt, dark slacks, and slim dark loafers. The shirt was casually opened at the throat to reveal a glowing bronze tan.

Almost at once he caught sight of her, and before Ted could reach her, Simon's long legs had covered the distance between them and he was at her side.

"March! I was about to look for you. I only just now found out from Stan that you were coming." His face was alight with pleasure and his dark eyes raked over her slim body in the clinging white dress. The cold knot of anxiety that had formed inside March dissolved swiftly as she felt a warmth take its place and radiate outward until every part of her was tingling with it. *Why do I let it affect me that way?* she scolded herself. *Why do I let his approval mean so much?* But then he was standing close to her, looking down at her and saying, "What happened to my little sea sprite? She seems to have disappeared. But the change is rather sensational, I must admit."

March smiled back at him but tried to hang onto her poise. "And this is all rather sensational, too. I've never been on a boat quite so elegant."

His eyes remained on her as though she had not spoken. With one finger he reached out to touch the flower behind her ear.

"By golly, there's the little lady!" a voice boomed from the cabin doorway. Startled, March turned to see Stan Massie, sun-reddened and hearty, his expensive-looking dress shirt open halfway to his waist to reveal several chains and a medallion. "There she is, everybody, and I want it to go on record right now as saying she's the best fishing expert in the islands, barring none. Honey, I take my hat off to you. All that stuff you told me about Great Guana Cay—you were right on the mark, with every bit of it." He came striding over to March just as the song ended and in the sudden stillness everyone stopped talking and stared. March felt herself blushing furiously as Stan gave her a hearty hug. "Only I hardly knew you, honey, all got up in that outfit. You're the best-looking fish expert *I've* ever met. Well, by golly, I got me a six-hundred-pound blue marlin, that's what I did. It's hanging in the hotel cooler right this minute. Took me two hours to land the fellow. Oh, he put up some battle, leapin' outa the water and fightin' me every inch of the way.''

"I'm glad you had good luck," March managed to say, and then suddenly she felt Simon's arm around her, protectively, and his voice interrupted Stan, "I was just about to show March around the boat, Stan."

"Oh great, you do that, Simon," Stan agreed loudly. "And give her something to eat, too. Nothin's too good for this little lady. Maybe later you'll give me some idea how I can get that fish of mine stuffed and mounted, honey. I'm gonna bring this one back with me or nobody in Texas is gonna believe I caught it."

"I don't know much about that," March smiled at him, feeling as she had the first time they met, that it was impossible to dislike anyone as hearty and friendly as Stan Massie. "Why don't you talk to Tommy Monday, the mechanic who's always around the dock? He'll know where to send you."

"Right you are. I'll do that. Say, you know you made this trip for me, Miss March? If it hadn't a been for you I'd a been out there still at Great Guana, probably havin' about as much luck as a kid with a string and a bent pin for a hook."

"See you later, Stan," Simon grinned, easing March away and guiding her toward the cabin. The musicians began to play their guitars again softly and the guests went back to their conversation, but several curious looks followed March and Simon as they left. Walking forward from the rear deck into the cabin they entered directly into a living room covered with a rich sand-colored carpet. Couches and chairs were arranged in small groupings, all of them uphol-stered in beach colors of blue and sand. There were glass-topped end tables and coffee tables. A writing desk stood against one wall. At the far forward end was the dining area, and for tonight, chairs had been removed from around the long dining table so that it could serve as a buffet. Beyond the table, which was laden with exotic-looking food, March had a glimpse of a galley area as a waiter pushed out through the door with a tray. She could see white-clad local help working there putting hors d'oeuvres on plates.

"Impressive, isn't it?" Simon commented.

"I've never seen anything like it. We have some fine big boats putting in at Coral Cay now and then, but never anything like this."

"Forward there, up beyond the galley, is the place where the captain sits to navigate."

"Does Mr. Massie captain his own boat?"

"He does. Rather surprising, isn't it? I mean, he doesn't give the impression of being that serious about it. But he is. And quite capable, too."

March turned and looked around her again, shaking her head in wonderment at the lavish decor, seemed less like a boat than a floating palace. She was acutely conscious all the while of Simon Wade's nearness. The touch of his hand on her elbow or at her back as he guided her sent flashes of warmth vibrating through her. *I must try to keep things impersonal*, she thought with a kind of desperation, and said lightly, "Are the Massies old friends of yours?"

"I have a place at Palm Beach, and so do they," he answered. "We're neighbors, you might say, at least on the occasions when both of us happen to be there at the same time."

March gave him a quick glance. "I see." It had startled her, hearing him say that. Once again she reflected on how strange it was for her to be here, and what a vast distance lay between her world and that of people like the Massies and Simon, who could speak so casually of "a place at Palm Beach." But even more, the words had such a definite sound. They conjured up a picture of a real house. And who was in

117

that house now while he was here on business interests? The woman who had traveled with him on the plane? Or perhaps the other woman whose name March had heard—Penny. And more, was one of them—could one of them—be Simon's wife? Stan Massie would know, of course, but March shied away from the thought of asking him. One thing she was sure of. Whole worlds lay between her and people whose beliefs, or lack of belief in general, placed them at such a distance from her. For a brief moment she thought about the emptiness of a life without the sustaining strength of Christ's love and wished it were possible to show this to Simon Wade. But could she ever make him see? Certainly there was no place in his life for someone like her. She was no more than a brief diversion for a man much more worldly and sophisticated than she. *I must be careful every step of the way*, she reminded herself. *I must not let my guard down again as I did yesterday on the reef.*

Someone waved at them from across the room and March was almost relieved to recognize Monica Massie, who at once made her way toward them. She was in a long, full gown of bright, shimmering material done in tropical colors. Its plunging V neckline exposed a glittering array of jewelry—all of it real, no doubt, March thought.

"Simon honey, I'm so glad you're taking care of Marge. Sweetie, my husband has been praising you until I'm just green with jealousy. He says you're the smartest thing he's ever met and that you know just everything there is to know about fish and oh, what is it? Reefs and things." Monica's two hands came out in a helpless gesture to indicate that her own expertise was in an entirely different direction. "Anyway, I'm just as glad as I can be that you were able to come tonight, and so's Caty. Now where is she anyway? Well, she's around here somewhere. Now look, Simon, you just take Marge right over to the table and give her something to eat. Honey, these local people make the best stuff!" She was edging them closer to the food. "Look there. Those are just the appetizers, do you believe it? That one there—" she pointed to a huge plate of hors d'oeuvre bread, colorfully spread—"that one's cream cheese, smoked salmon, sliced scallion, and dill, all mixed together, isn't that unbelievable? And that one—" her hand flashed diamonds as she pointed again—"that one's sweet butter, shrimp, lettuce, black caviar, and hard-boiled egg yolk. I know because I asked them what it was. It's heavenly, too. Now you just have some and make yourself at home, sweetie. You take good care of her, Simon, you hear?"

She moved away from them, her colorful skirt fluttering out behind her. March stole a glance at Simon and found him looking down at her with an expression of conspiratorial amusement.

"I'm afraid we'll never get her to understand about the name. She's got it in her head that you're Marge, and I doubt if she'd listen anyway."

"I don't mind," March answered. "I rather like her." Surprisingly, she found this to be true. There was a brassy quality, a showiness about Monica Massie, but a rather direct honesty too, she suspected. Caitlin was the puzzling one. And where was Caitlin tonight?

"Why is it, by the way?" Simon asked suddenly.

"Why is what?"

"Why is it March? How did you happen to be named that?"

"I was born in March, during a huge storm that found its way into the record books, so they tell me. High winds and enormous seas, that sort of thing."

"It's a good name for you then. Very appropriate for a sea sprite."

March turned hastily toward the buffet table and began exclaiming over it. It was indeed impressive.

Monica's effusive descriptions had only scratched the surface. March saw a variety of other hors d'oeuvres—turkey with grated carrots, tomato, chopped walnuts; asparagus spears were rolled up in ham and topped with pimiento. Instead of the customary green salad there was a richly colored mix of avacado, broccoli and red pepper in a bowl, all dressed with vinaigrette. For the main course, fresh fish had been grilled and now nestled on a huge silver platter surrounded by braised fennel and cut tomatoes. It was garnished with a stripe of lemon slices down its center, and a feathering of dill. Grilled pork lion had been marinated, roasted, chilled and thinly sliced, and there were side dishes to go with it of mango or peach chutney.

"You must have something," Simon said. "Monica will have my hide if I don't take care of you."

"Everything's so beautiful," March said. "The boat, the table—"

"You look lovely yourself, March," Caitlin said, and although the compliment rolled off easily, it seemed to March there was a faint tightening around the girl's mouth as she said it, as though it might have cost her an effort. Caitlin's eyes took in the clinging white dress, the slender shoulders lightly touched with sun, the white flower in March's hair. "Well, do have fun," she said briskly. "I must say hello to people. Simon, be sure to introduce March around, won't you?"

"Yes, of course," he said, but when Caitlin had turned away he murmured, "Will you be angry if I don't?"

"Don't?"

"Introduce you to people? Keep you to myself?"

Color flared across March's cheekbones and she avoided his eyes briefly. All her resolves about staying aloof, all her insistence that she would put him out of her mind, all her denials to Paulie and to

120

herself, flashed through her in a searing moment. She knew them to be false, every one of them. And yet she knew equally well that nothing but heartbreak lay ahead of her if she let herself give in to this emotion that had invaded her body, mind, and spirit. She would be as vulnerable as any school girl, and as painfully hurt. He was worldly, experienced, no doubt easily bored; even more, he might very well be married. And she was a novelty to him. More than anything she must keep their relationship light and superficial. She had been wrong to let her feelings show yesterday on the reef. She would not repeat the mistake. She looked up at him and said brightly, "Well, you did promise me there was more of the boat to see. Could we do that now?"

His dark eyes held her blue ones fast for an instant as though he sought some answer or tried to read deep inside her. Then he said pleasantly, "Certainly. Right this way."

The remainder of the evening was, for March, a kaleidoscope of colors and impressions. The rooms below deck were all open and lighted for guests to wander through. March found them astonishing. The master bedroom was carpeted in violet, with a furry white bedspread on the king-sized bed – Monica's taste, March guessed. On the bedside table was a wedding photo of Stan and her, ornately framed. Their bath had a silver shower curtain. Caitlin's room, which also had its own bath, was more tasteful, done in shades of apricot, with subdued lighting and a simple silk bedspread. There were two other bedrooms with a bath between them. Some of the guests were using these to freshen up. When March and Simon went back upstairs and sampled some of the delicacies she realized she was used to Miss Emily's subtler cooking techniques. Only when fruit was brought around on trays—ripe strawberries, honeydew, and pineapple dipped in honey and lemon juice, threaded on skewers, then frozen and served tingling cold—was she tempted, and this, she had to admit, was delicious.

At around ten o'clock the two musicians left and Caitlin and Ted promptly activated the stereo. The music became a more immediate presence at the party, filtering through speakers placed in both the cabin and on the rear deck. Coupled with the rising tone of conversation as guests grew more animated with laughter and exclamations, it gave the whole gathering a noisier air. Talk became difficult, and March was content to watch and listen. Once when one of March's island records was playing, Simon bent close to her ear and said, "That's a marvelous record. I wonder where Caitlin got it." March said, "It's mine," but he had already straightened up and did not hear her. Still, she was pleased that he liked it. At last he shouted down at her, "I don't think it's going to get much quieter around here. Shall we walk out on the dock for a few minutes?"

March nodded and started to move away with him, pushing toward the open doorway to the deck. The record ended then, and March glanced across the cabin and saw Caitlin leaning over to change it. Ted was with her and it seemed to March they were having a disagreement. Ted said something to her and his expression was angry, but Caitlin gave him what looked like a sharp answer and went on with what she was doing.

Sound came through the speakers again, swelling and throbbing in an introduction March recognized. Gina Leigh—her favorite. She waited for the voice to come in—sultry, dramatic, full of the pain and glory of lost love. She looked up at Simon, hoping to see a response in him. *Even though we can never be anything to each other*, she thought, *it would be nice to think that he liked something I like*. She froze with apprehension as she saw the look on his face. He had

122

gone white under his tan, and his mouth was a thin bitter line. He turned toward the stereo, his forehead drawn into a look of fury. At the same moment March became aware that much of the conversation in the room had stopped, leaving only the throbbing, husky voice, and that covert looks were being directed toward the two of them. Without a word Simon left her side and crossed the carpeted room in a half dozen long strides. With cold deliberation he removed the needle from the record and in the almost total silence that ensued, said angrily to Caitlin, "Who's responsible for this?"

Caitlin looked concerned, her face a study in contrition and apology. "Oh, Simon dear, I'm so terribly sorry. I just didn't think. The records are March's, and she said this was her particular favorite. She especially wanted me to play it tonight." Her voice drifted off as she looked at him, her mouth formed into an appealing pout that begged forgiveness. March, who had heard her words in the silent room, could feel a cold paralysis creeping over her as she realized that something was terribly, irrevocably wrong. Caitlin's small lie did not bother her. All she could see was the look on Simon's face—stony anger, and the faint tension of a muscle that moved tautly in his lean cheek.

Without another word to Caitlin he turned and walked back to March, seizing her by the elbow and pushed her roughly out of the cabin and onto the deck. He propelled her up onto the short gangplank and onto the dock, then dragged her along the dock, out toward the darkened end, away from the lights and the music that had started up again. March quivered, trembling with remorse even though she did not know what she had done. She stifled a sob and looked up at him. In the darkness his face was pale and indistinct, but she did not need to see to recognize the boiling fury of it. Fear stabbed at her as she almost anticipated physical violence from him. But it was his voice that lashed her.

"What do you mean—doing a thing like that to me?"

"But what did I—"

"Playing along with me yesterday, acting friendly. You've hated me right from the beginning, haven't you?"

"No—really I haven't—"

"It's that precious island of yours, isn't it? You're sore at me over that. You regard it as your personal property and you hate me for laying a finger on it. Or on you. You couldn't wait to get back at me, could you? Well, too bad, lady, because it's my island now and I'll do with it what I please. As for laying a finger on you, you can be sure I won't. Not after tonight."

And before March could answer again or protest he had seized her and pulled her against him so tightly that his arms seemed to hold her in a grip of steel. His mouth came down upon hers, not with the tenderness she had felt before, but bruisingly, cruelly. One hand came up to grip her hair and she could feel it coming loose from its twist and the white hibiscus blossom pulling out and falling to the dock. She pressed her palms wildly against his chest, pushing as hard as she could, but her strength was no match for his. When at last he released her she thrust herself away from him, gasping for breath and hearing him say, "Just something to remember me by, lady."

Outraged, bewilderingly accused of something she could not understand, March felt a helpless anger welling up in her. Without thinking or reasoning she took a step toward him, brought her hand up and struck him across the face with her open palm. "Don't you ever come near me again!" she raged. "Don't you dare!"

He looked at her for a moment in the sudden stillness.

"Just great," he said flatly, and even in the dim light she could see the sardonic twist of his mouth. "The final touch. You couldn't have done it better if you'd rehearsed it. Or did you?"

And without another word he turned and strode away from her along the dock toward shore. March watched him go, her breath still coming in tight gasps, her heart pounding. Then slowly, achingly, she leaned down and picked up the mangled white blossom. For a long time she stood there holding it, hearing the distant laughter and music of the party. She could feel the painful throbbing of her mouth and moistened it gingerly with her tongue, but all she could taste was her own salt tears.

Several minutes must have passed—but March had lost track of time – when she sensed that she was no longer alone. She felt too weary and defeated even to turn around. And then a quiet voice said, "You look as if you could use a friend. May I walk you home?"

Ted Newburn's voice was so kind and full of sympathy that March felt like melting against him and letting him take care of her. *I'm so tired of being strong*, she thought wretchedly. *I'm so tired of saying I'm all right, don't worry about me*.

"Thank you," she whispered. "Please take me home."

CHAPTER 8

"NO, PLEASE DON'T BOTHER. I'm very good at this, I assure you," Ted said as he rummaged through March's small neat kitchen, finding both the coffee and electric percolator. He put water in the pot, measured coffee expertly and let it start perking. March, who had protested at first and then tried to help, sank into a chair at the kitchen table, giving into an inertia that had suddenly sapped every ounce of her energy.

"I'm so sorry," she said, feeling wretched. "I hate coming all apart this way. Putting you to so much trouble, making you leave the party. But really, I'm all right now. You should get back to your friends. I'm okay."

He ignored her protests. "Trying to get rid of me?" he smiled. He slipped out of his light jacket, rolled his shirtsleeves up and began searching through shelves for cups. When he had found them he placed them on the counter beside the pot and waited while the perking went on and the little house began to smell fragrantly of fresh-brewed coffee.

"No, of course I'm not trying to get rid of you," March said, trying to smile. "It was awfully nice of you to walk me all the way up here." A thought struck her. "I didn't even say goodnight to the Massies. They'll think I'm dreadful."

"You can't do anything wrong in Stan's eyes, I promise. And Monica takes such things very casually."

"But it isn't right for me to drag you away from your friends."

"Look here now. That's enough," he said firmly. "I'm here because I want to be. Do you know how many of those parties I go to and how glad I am to be missing this one? Now why don't you change into something you'll be comfortable in and I'll bring the coffee in to the living room."

March looked down at the white dress and realized what Ted had already seen—that it felt all wrong and she was suddenly miserable in it.

"All right," she said wearily. "Thank you, I believe I will change." She pushed herself up from the table and left the kitchen. In the bathroom she scrubbed her face and toweled it vigorously, then brushed out her hair. In her own room she changed from the white dress to a pair of soft yellow slacks and a light-weight white sweater, for the evening was cooler now. She slipped into yellow espadrilles that matched her slacks and returned to the living room, where Ted was just carrying in the coffee and placing the tray on the low table. She could see by his approving expression that she looked better, and some of the lethargy she had felt before seemed to be lifting. She managed a small smile.

"You certainly are a very handy fellow," she observed.

"Perhaps I should do this for a living."

She glanced at him, trying to read past his flippancy, wondering how much he had observed of the scene between Simon and her on the dock. Had he been watching the whole time—or overhearing it all? Once again the humiliation and pain of it swept over her and she sank down on the couch with a tired sigh. He gave her a shrewd appraising look and said suddenly, "You don't know much about Simon, do you?"

"Oh please," she whispered. "I don't want to talk about it."

"Then suppose I do the talking."

"No, really. There's no need. Or if there's any talking to be done, he's the one who should do it. I still have no idea what happened back there."

"I intend to speak to him."

"No, there's no need for that either," she said quickly. "I mean, it doesn't matter to me what he thinks or what crazy ideas he has about me. We're nothing to each other, and that's a good way to leave it."

"Drink your coffee," he said gently, and she picked up the cup in both her hands and drank it hot and steaming, feeling a little of her strength coming back. "I think some sort of explanation is due you. It's Caitlin's fault, really, what happened, but it's mine, too, because I should have stopped her."

March looked at him over the rim of her cup, not understanding but wondering whether anything short of physical restraint would ever stop Caitlin from doing anything she had her mind set on. And once again Ted seemed to be reading her thoughts. "Not an easy thing to do, granted. Well, look, there's more to it than that. And I'd better start further back." He took the chair opposite her and drank from his cup. Then he put it down and sat leaning forward, his hands loosely clasped between his knees.

"Eight years ago Simon was in Italy working on his first big job after he had just formed his own company on a shoestring. He was something of a boy wonder in those days, all nerve and talent and ambition, and he'd landed a contract to do a resort hotel and some other smaller buildings along with it in a little seaside town southwest of Rome. One of those picturesque little places with Roman ruins and hillside houses and a sixteenth century church and so on. Some wealthy industrialist from northern Italy was putting up the money—well, that's beside the point. What matters was that there was a movie company working on location there, and a beautiful Italian film star, Giovanna Bellini, was acting in the movie. And—" Ted spread his hands. "There was instant chemistry between them. He fell for her with all the impetuousness and lack of thought that most young guys show in the face of overwhelming beauty. And she— well, she reacted to his admiration and his good looks—he's pretty impressive himself in that department—"

"I know," March murmured, and Ted glanced at her.

"So that was it. Within six weeks they were married. She finished her picture and he went on to finish his hotel, and within months both of them had scored big successes. It looked as if the whole world was theirs on a platter. He began to get a lot of notice for his work and producers began to pound on her door. Still no problem, because when a big offer came to her from America, it went along well with his plans to return. And it didn't stop there. Their two careers went shooting ahead on parallel courses. He began to have his pick of the choice jobs and she got the lead in a Broadway show and then a movie deal, recording contracts and so on. She Americanized her name—"

"Gina Leigh," March said softly. "But her own name was so beautiful – Giovanna Bellini."

"Her manager talked her into it. Just as he talked her into running off to Europe with him two years later. That's when she was killed—when his private plane crashed in the Alps."

"I remember when she was killed," March said. "It seemed so terribly sad, and such a waste. . .all that wonderful talent. It must have been awful for Simon. Yet their life together—" She hesitated, and Ted's eyebrows went up, questioning. "Well, it must have been so hollow," she went on. "I mean with nothing, no values, to hold onto. Nothing to give meaning to it." She knew what she meant. The picture of the little church in the clearing and all it had meant in her own life was uppermost in her mind, but it was hard to express such thoughts to someone as worldly as Ted. And there was another thought nudging at her, an aspect of Simon's character that had been unknown to her earlier. Clearly he had never forgiven Gina. And that unforgiving heart with its grievance jealously nurtured, could in time destroy the very fabric of his life. Refusal to forgive was corrosive, destructive, March knew.

"Still, you can imagine how he must have felt, hearing that record tonight."

Sympathy, which had been March's first impulsive response, was replaced by cold resentment as the scene on the dock came back to her. She felt the crushing cruelty of that mouth on hers, the steely grip of the hand on her hair—most of all the bitter arrogance of the man himself, taking his own hurt out on her. Conscience stabbed at her. Was she not falling short herself? She had not yet found forgiveness in her heart for Simon, had she?

"I can see how he might have felt, yes," she said coolly, "but I don't feel it's any excuse for his acting as he did. How could he possibly have thought I'd do such a thing on purpose— even assuming Caitlin had told the truth—how could he have assumed that I knew of any connection between him and Gina Leigh?"

Ted looked at her with a trace of amusement. "I would have thought the whole world knew about Gina Leigh's life and loves."

"Well, I didn't," March said firmly. "International gossip isn't the everyday concern of a place like Coral Cay. We're a bit backward here, I'm afraid. And besides, he must hear her records all the time. They're still played everywhere. He should be used to it."

"But not at a private party, not among friends. And most certainly not as a deliberate jab meant to hurt, which is the way he must have seen it."

"I don't care how he saw it," March said. "He was unfair and arrogant and cruel."

"Perhaps. But not wholly to blame. Caitlin and I were the ones at fault. I'm afraid Caitlin's pretty thoughtless sometimes."

Pretty thoughtless was certainly a major understatement, March thought. But Ted himself was being kind, and as they sat companionably in March's cosy living room, drinking coffee and talking together quietly, she began to feel an unwinding within herself, a relaxing that she knew she owed to him. Only deep inside her at the very center of her being, a small hard core of resentment still lay and refused to soften or go away. Nor did March really want it to, for around it she was building her decision. No more delays, no more lame excuses for postponement. It was time now—and Simon Wade had furnished ample motivation tonight—for her to leave the islands for good.

Later at the door Ted bent to kiss her cheek gently and asked, "Sure you'll be all right now?" March nodded and managed a smile and a firm answer. "Don't worry about me. I'll be fine now." As she closed the door on him a fleeting thought came to her. If there had been no Simon Wade, if Ted had been the only one I met here on Coral Cay, what would I have felt for him?

When she woke the next morning she lay staring at the ceiling for a moment, remembering the night before. Then she pushed it out of her mind firmly, swung both legs out of bed and sat on the edge deciding what to do first. From now on there would be no hiding in the house, no avoiding the places where she might run into him. If they met, they would meet as casual acquaintances. There would be no more to it than that. And the first thing she had to do was talk business with Don Sanders.

She went into the kitchen, washed the coffee pot, which she had left on the counter the night before, and put fresh coffee on to perk. Then she showered and dressed, putting on a sea-green cotton skirt, white eyelet top and sandals. She returned to the kitchen to have juice, toast, and coffee, and when she had washed the dishes and tidied the kitchen she went into the bedroom and made her bed. She hung the white dress from the night before in the farthest corner of the closet. When she was satisfied that everything was neat—she must keep it in good order from now on in case prospective buyers wanted to see it—she went out the front door, closing it firmly behind her and walking down the path to the hotel. Out in the marina she could see that some of the big boats belonging to the Massies' party guests were pulling out.

Paulie was just leaving as she ran up the front steps of the inn.

"Oh, March, I wanted to hear all about the party," she wailed. "Only I have to take Miss Emily's big dough mixer to Johnsville and see if Jasper Forty can fix it right today. Something's blown out and she's beside herself."

"Can't Tommy fix it? He can make anything run."

"I'm sure he could, only he's not here. He went out early in his boat—took Simon Wade to Whispering Pines Cay. That Ted Newburn went with them. Oh, March, I know how you feel about that. I mean, you haven't said much about it, but I know you hate the idea of Whispering Pines being all built up. I hope you're not mad at Tommy for taking him."

"Of course not."

"It's just that Tommy can use the money—you know."

"I know. And it's perfectly all right, honestly."

"Look, wouldn't you like to ride along with me? Then you could tell me all about last night."

The longer she could put that off the better, March thought.

"I'd like to, Paulie, but I have to speak to your dad about some business. Is he terribly rushed?"

"No, he just went in to have coffee. You can catch him in the dining room."

"See you later then." March turned and hurried up the steps, feeling a little freer now that she knew she would not run the risk of meeting Simon. She found Don Sanders at the family table in the dining room, relaxing with coffee and a newspaper. There were late breakfasters sitting at a few tables, but the early morning rush was over. Sunshine filtering through the trees outside the windows made a dappled pattern of light and shadows in the room. Breakfast place mats on the tables were of woven grass and were in bright shades of yellow, pink, orange, green, and everything had a polished look about it, even though there were scars here and there on the wooden table tops. It all wore a homey look of comfort. March supposed that was why so many of the guests were repeaters, coming here year after year. Mentally she compared it to the great concrete-and-glass edifice that would soon be built on Whispering Pines.

"Good morning, Uncle Don," she said, sliding into a seat opposite him.

He looked up over his reading glasses, mildly surprised.

"Well! Thought you'd be sleeping late this morning. I hear you were mingling with the jet set last night."

"Oh, Uncle Don, I don't think they even call it that any more," she teased, turning away inquiries. "I

133

have to talk to you for a minute, if you're not too busy."

He dropped his newspaper onto the table. "I'm all yours."

"Well, when we talked a few nights ago about my selling the house and boat, you said go slowly, don't be in a hurry and so on. But now I have thought it over, and I do want to go ahead with it. So I need your advice on what to do first. Should I see a real estate agent in Johnsville, or what?"

Don Sanders took his reading glasses off slowly and looked sober. "I had a feeling we'd have to deal with that soon. I know you when your mind's made up."

"I know. Just like father," she smiled, trying to keep the conversation light.

"Yes. Well, there's a lot of truth there. But the thing is, March, I did have it on my mind, and I've been giving it some thought. Do you remember the Hollisters? They've come here for vacations for ten years or so."

"Yes, I remember them. They used to charter our boat often and have Dad take them around the islands. In fact, I went along a couple of times."

Don nodded. "He's an investment banker in New York, but he's retiring after this year. This'll be his last vacation with us, he said, because what he wants to do is buy a place here. On Coral Cay if he can find one, or over on Coral Island if he can't. But Coral Cay's the place they really want to be."

March's heart lurched uneasily as she guessed what Don's next words would be.

"I was wondering if they might be interested in your house."

In spite of herself, March felt she had to offer argument.

"But an invesment banker—that sounds like money. Would they be satisfied with anything as modest as my little place?"

"Oh, I guess they're well fixed, but they don't seem to have lavish tastes. I mean—they've come back to this place year after year." Don gave a nod around the pleasant, well-worn dining room. "Anyway, it would be worth asking, wouldn't it—if you really do want to sell?" He emphasized the *if*, and March realized he had noticed her hesitation.

"Oh, I do," she said at once. "Definitely. And I think it's a wonderful idea. When are they coming?"

"They're due in today. Want me to speak to them about it?"

"Yes. I'd appreciate it, Uncle Don," March said decisively. "And I'll be glad to show them the house any time they like."

"They might even be interested in your boat," Don said. "It's not difficult to manage, and it's in good shape."

"Yes. They might," March said in a small voice, and for some reason this idea hit her even harder than the prospect of selling the house. The *Flower of the Sea,* the captain's boat—now hers—the thought of it belonging to strangers was like a knife turning in her heart.

Marian Sanders came bustling in from the kitchen, looking distraught, but brightening into a smile at the sight of March.

"Oh, March honey, how nice to see you. Paulie's not here, I'm afraid – "

"I just saw her, Aunt Marian."

"Oh good. Well, we all want to hear about the party, only what a morning! You heard about Miss Emily's mixer—"

"Paulie told me."

"I've had quite a time with her—Miss Emily. She wants to do the fresh bread by hand, but I told her to just eliminate it for one day until we get the mixer working." Marian's reading glasses bounced on their chain against her plump bosom. She seized them and

135

put them on her nose so that she could examine a sheaf of papers she held. "Don, will the Hollisters mind if we put them in Fifteen instead of Nine? Nine's the one we usually give them because it's a corner room and they like it."

"Well, Fifteen's a corner room too," Don observed mildly. "They can see the same ocean out of those windows. Besides, the Hollisters are very agreeable. Why can't they have Nine?" he asked as an afterthought.

"It was spoken for yesterday by that Mr. Wade. And Paulie took the reservation. I don't believe she realized the Hollisters would be here today."

"Is he changing his room?" Don frowned.

"No, it's for a lady," Marian said a little stiffly. "He asked for Number Nine especially." She consulted her papers again. "A Miss Miranda Thompson. She's arriving today, too. It's to go on his bill. She's to be his guest."

"Might be a secretary or assistant—someone who works for his firm," Don said.

"I hardly think so," Marian said, and her voice was touched with scorn at male naïveté. "You don't *select* a room for a secretary, not if it's business. You just reserve it."

And Paulie knew it last night when I was dressing in her room, March thought. *Miss Emily too. That look they exchanged—both of them worried that I might be going head over heels for someone who had already invited another woman here.*

"Besides," Marian added meaningfully, "Number Nine adjoins his room."

The knife March had already felt in her heart took another turn.

By midafternoon she had changed into shorts, shirt, and sneakers and gone to the dock to clean up the *Flower of the Sea*. She had not bothered to do her customary housekeeping after they had snorkeled at the reef two days before. Now pangs of memory assaulted her as she picked up the scattered equipment—breathing masks and flippers—that had been tossed down helter-skelter in the boat when they finished. She packed them in her dive bag and set it on the dock to carry home. Then she gave her attention to other chores, coiling up and stowing away lines, sponging the deck, then easing the boat around to the other side of the dock and filling up the gas tanks, another job she had neglected to do. Tommy Monday always told her it was important to top off the tanks in an older boat, even one as well cared for as hers; sludge could form and dirt choke the gas line if the level of fuel went too low. The knowledge of why she had neglected all these things lay searing and painful in the back of her mind as she worked. The feeling of Simon's arms around her as they clung to the boat and to each other in the sun-warmed turquoise water, the enveloping kiss, full of passion and promise, all mocked her painfully now. But perhaps pain was what she needed, she told herself, to stiffen her spine, to cure her indecisiveness.

She was back at her berth at the dock when she saw Tommy's boat come in – a well cared for older boat of about the same size as hers. Tommy stopped at the gas pump to refill his own tanks, and March saw Ted and Simon getting out and climbing up onto the dock. It was a quiet time at the marina. Most of the tourists were either out fishing or, in the case of the older guests, sitting on the veranda of the inn. Some of those with young children were on the small strip of sandy beach further along the shoreline. Besides March's boat, the *Ayes of Texas* rode quietly at its berth. Stan Massie had gone off fishing again, and she knew Caitlin and Monica had risen late and then gone off somewhere. She had seen them leave in a boat that must have belonged to one of their guests who had stayed overnight in it after the party. Hired help and crew members had been busy until an hour or so before, cleaning the yacht, taking down and putting away strings of lights, mopping the decks and polishing the brightwork.

She glanced up as Ted and Simon approached. Ted smiled at her and waved, but did not stop to talk as he swung up onto the Massie's boat. Simon looked down at her, hesitated, then took a step nearer. March turned away and gave her attention to the tarpaulin, which she was just unfolding in order to cover the boat.

"Could I give you a hand with that?"

She did not look up. "No thanks. I can manage."

Out of the corner of her eye she saw him glance at the bag of diving equipment that she had tossed on the dock. She noticed, before looking away hurriedly, that he had a roll of blueprints under his arm.

"How are things on your island?" she asked tartly.

"Fine." She could feel that he was hesitating. Then suddenly he dropped down into the boat with her. The *Flower* rocked easily under his weight. "Do you mind?" he asked. "That is, I didn't request permission to come aboard. I believe that's customary."

"It is," she said. "But then, when did you ever worry about the small amenities?"

"I guess I was afraid you wouldn't let me on—or maybe you'd have me hung from the yardarm."

"Not the worst idea you've ever had," she said, facing him at last.

He scanned her face, and his own looked drawn and intense. "March, I want to apologize for last night. Ted talked to me this morning, but I'm such a fool. I should have known without being told that you'd never do anything like that intentionally."

"Apology accepted," she snapped. "Is that all?"

"You accept my apology but you haven't really forgiven me, is that it?"

"You can put it any way you like. I don't think we have anything more to say to each other."

"But won't you give me a chance to make it up to you?"

"There's nothing to make up. Just forget it." Yet even as she said it, March was aware of the nearness of him. He was standing close enough for her to see the muscles under his knit shirt, the hairs on his tanned forearms that were bleaching now in the sun. The sea breeze ruffled his dark hair and sent a curling strand of it across his forehead.

"I would hate to throw away a friendship that was just getting under way," he said softly.

"There was nothing getting under way between us," she said stonily. "You belong in one world and I belong in another. It's as simple as that." She was more than ever convinced of this since hearing about the impending arrival of Miranda Thompson. Like the beautiful Diana of the plane trip, like the sultry Caitlin, like the glamorous and tragic Gina Leigh, this was another in a long and seemingly endless parade of women in his life. She went on coldly, "You have one set of values and I have another. You have one sort of friends and mine are quite different. I don't belong in your world or the Massies'. I didn't belong at that party last night. And I'd appreciate it if you'd stay away from me from now on. I won't be on Coral Cay much longer. It shouldn't be hard for us to stay out of each other's way."

"I suppose I deserve some of that, but not all," he said grimly, and she could see the muscle in his cheek twitching as though in anger. *Good enough*, she thought. *If I've been unfair, it's no more than he was last night. And there's no way to end this thing except to end it, once and for all.*

"Do you mind?" she said, beginning to fit the tarpaulin over the boat and fasten the grommets that held it in place. "I'd like to finish up here."

He gave her a long look that seemed to search her face and to probe even further, behind her eyes, into her most secret thoughts. She turned deliberately and did not look after him as he vaulted lightly up from the boat onto the dock. She could hear his long stride pounding along the boards as she finished covering the boat. When she picked up the snorkeling equipment and headed toward shore he was nowhere to be seen. *I have fallen short again*, March thought, trying to take a probing inward look at her own heart, but finding still no forgiveness there. Paulie's little car was parked in its spot at the side of the inn, however, so March deposited the bag near the kitchen door and went in.

The kitchen was in a state of well-organized uproar, with Miss Emily moving purposefully from one job to another and calling out orders as she went. A teenage boy, a nephew of Tiny the waiter, was cleaning vegetables at a counter against one wall, and Paulie herself was dashing about in a huge white apron, following Miss Emily's bidding.

"Got the mixer fixed," she explained in a rush to March, "but it's put the kitchen a couple of hours behind, so I'm pitching in."

"'Bout as much good in the kitchen as a winter overcoat," Miss Emily grumbled, "but I had to have another pair of hands."

"Well look, maybe there's something I can do," March volunteered.

Paulie shot her a wink. "Don't listen to Miss Emily, March. Actually things are in very good order here— largely due to my expert assistance. But you might ask Mom if she needs any help. I saw the taxi leave for the airport, so guests ought to be arriving soon." She gave March a tentative, questioning look.

"Including a Miss Thompson, I hear," March said, keeping her tone light.

"March, I wanted to tell you, but I wasn't sure how you felt about him, I mean."

"Butter," Miss Emily ordered sternly. "And that pot over there."

"Talk to you later, March," Paulie said, lugging the heavy iron pot cheerfully to Miss Emily and saying in a teasing voice, "What would you do without me, Miss E?"

March waved and went out through the now empty dining room and into the lobby. But Marian Sanders, behind the desk was calm and efficient. "All in order, dear," she sang out in answer to March's offer of help. "I put on a couple of extra girls this afternoon—Tiny's nieces—to do up beds, and we're ready for everything now."

March glanced around and walked slowly toward the front door and the veranda. She pushed the screen open and saw that there were the usual few tourists relaxing and chatting there, but no sign of Simon Wade, so she edged out quietly. Don Sanders, who was leaning against the railing talking with a guest, caught sight of her, waved a hand in greeting and went on with his conversation. March made her way to the far corner of the veranda, smiling at guests along the way. She moved a chair back against the wall in the most inconspicuous spot she could find and sat on the edge of it. She would like to see the Hollisters when they arrived, she explained to herself, knowing even as she framed the thought that it was not the reason she was there. It was Miranda Thompson who had excited a burning curiosity in her.

The island's one taxi, a sagging, rust-pocked van, pulled up a few minutes later, and Ed Beaslie, the owner, got out to help the new arrivals with their luggage. Don Sanders went down the steps to greet them, and there was a general sharpening of interest on the part of the veranda-sitters. March recognized the Hollisters at once, a pleasant-looking couple past middle age, obviously pleased to be back in a place they enjoyed. Don Sanders greeted them warmly and helped them with their bags. Two women followed them out of the van, vacationers in their forties, both

141

wearing sturdy shoes and and looking about with interest. Neither of them was Miranda Thompson, March was sure.

Then another woman, younger looking, perhaps in her early thirties, got out of the car. March regarded her curiously. She was simply dressed in a lightweight beige suit. Her brown hair was cut short and close to her head. She was trim and slender. Attractive, March thought, although her face was turned away for the moment. Then she turned her head so that March had a better view of her. It was a face that did not seem to go with the rest of her, for it was drawn into a frown that looked like a perpetual one. She had a thin, severe mouth, two vertical forehead lines and sharp gray eyes that darted about critically as though nothing she saw quite measured up to her expectations. But no one else seemed to be getting out; it must be Miranda Thompson. An odd attachment for Simon Wade, she thought—a man she knew to be passionate and warm-blooded, even though, as she reminded herself, he had other less attractive attributes.

Then, as March watched, the woman turned back to the car and held out a hand, and her words came quite clearly.

"All right, Penny, come along. This is it, apparently."

A young girl—a child of seven or so—jumped out of the car, disdaining the proffered hand. March's breath drew in sharply with surprise. For the child standing there, sturdy and long-legged in khaki shorts, looked enough like Simon to be a mirror image. *Or his child*, March thought with a shock. Ted never mentioned a child, but there could have been one. She looked again, and this time could see like a transparency overlaying the features that were so much Simon's, another look, a glow in the brown eyes, a gleaming sheen in the dark curls of close-cropped hair, a slightly softer, rosier look about the mouth. *She is Gina Leigh's child, too*, March thought. Giovanna Bellini's child. And as she studied the oval face with its pale olive skin through which a rosy glow appeared under the cheekbones, it seemed to March it resembled faces she had seen in paintings by the Italian masters. Even with the practical shorts and healthy bounciness, the little girl's beauty was apparent.

There was a flurry at the door as it banged open and Simon came hurrying out of the hotel and down the steps.

"Penny!" he called out and her face lighted up at the sight of him.

"Daddy!" He picked her up and her arms went around his neck. Her sneakered feet met at his back as she twined her legs around him.

"What a hug! There now, hold on, lady—that's some grip. Did you like the flight from Florida? Didn't scare you, did it, out over the ocean in that little plane?"

"Daddy! I'm never scared."

"All right now, down you go. Miss Thompson, delighted to see you." His tone grew more formal as he held out a hand to the woman.

"How do you do, Mr. Wade."

"I'm sure you'd like to go directly to your room."

" *I* wouldn't," Penny said.

"All right, you," he said, but the look he gave the child was suffused with love. "But I'm sure Miss Thompson would like to unpack and rest before dinner. I've reserved a very pleasant corner room for you and Penny, Miss Thompson."

"I daresay everything will be quite satisfactory," Miss Thompson said, her tone indicating that she was putting a brave face on it, but that she regarded the hotel as not quite up to her standards. "Vacationers must be prepared to rough it a bit, of course."

As they turned and walked up the veranda steps March shrank back in her chair, wishing herself smaller and out of sight, fearful that he might turn and look her way. Seeing her there he would guess at her curiosity, would take it as a sign of renewed interest on her part. He crossed the veranda and held the door open for Miss Thompson to precede him. His daughter clung tightly to his hand and chattered away, and not once did he look in March's direction. Indeed, he seemed unaware of anyone around him. The two were in a world of their own. The words repeated themselves in March's head—*a world of their own* —and she swallowed painfully as she heard the screen door slam behind them. Somewhere inside her March seemed to hear an echo of the sound, as though a door had slammed on a part of her life too.

CHAPTER 9

"So GLAD YOU COULD JOIN US, Miss Raffin," Mr. Hollister said. He and his wife both smiled as March approached their table and Mr. Hollister got up to hold her chair for her. March had dressed for dinner in a pale blue sundress that highlighted her deepening golden tan.

"It was good of you to ask me," she said. Don Sanders had relayed the Hollisters' invitation to March after speaking with them earlier.

"We were shocked when we heard the news from Don Sanders about Captain Raffin," Mrs. Hollister said.

"Yes. Terrible, terrible . . . " Mr. Hollister said, his voice drifting off helplessly.

"Only last spring when we were here he took us around in his boat and made the time so pleasant for us," Mrs. Hollister said gently.

"I know he always looked forward to your visits," March said, meaning it. "I think because he knew you were both so fond of the islands."

"Indeed we are," the older woman said.

"And now Don tells us you're thinking of selling your house," Mr. Hollister said.

"More than just thinking. I'm really going to."

Mr. Hollister shook his head sadly. "Well, I certainly am sorry to hear that Coral Cay will be losing you. However, I suppose it gets down to a matter of hard realities, and that's what we want to discuss with you. Don mentioned a price that sounds fair to us, if the house is all he claims."

"It's small," March said, feeling the need to be honest, "but it's always been well cared for. I'd be glad to show it to you tomorrow, or any time you say."

"Good. Let's say tomorrow, late in the morning perhaps?"

"Fine."

"Don mentioned that your boat will be for sale as well."

In spite of herself March hesitated briefly. Then she said with firmness, "Yes, I'll be selling the boat too."

"We've spent so many happy hours on it," Mrs. Hollister said.

"Of course I'm not the seaman your dad was," Mr. Hollister said, "but since we'll be spending more time here—we plan to live here at least eight months of the year—perhaps we'll have time to learn and gain some experience."

"Of course," March agreed. "You know Tommy Monday, and he'd be only too glad to help you keep the boat in good running order too."

Both of them were looking at her, and March could feel their genuine kindness struggling with their obvious pleasure at having found exactly what they had been looking for. She tried to put them at ease.

"You'd be making things much easier for me," she said. "If you find the house suits you, that is. And I would be so relieved at knowing someone like you two had the house and boat. I know you'd take good care of both of them."

"Yes, of course we would, my dear," Mrs. Hollister said warmly, and put her hand on top of March's in a friendly gesture. As if sealing the bargain, March thought, and wondered why it caused her such a pang of melancholy when it was exactly what she had been hoping for. It seemed to her she could see her whole past slipping away from her like sand running through a sieve. All the blue and golden days of her growing up, all the scent-filled, moon-silvered nights on Coral Cay. The sea, the tides, the cloudless skies, all the storms and passions of tropical weather. All gone, all behind her now. Everything that had made her March Raffin was disappearing. And Simon—he too was vanishing—a dream she should never have let herself dream. *Better off*, she told herself sternly. I'm better off. From now on, no more looking back.

They went on chatting then as the dining room began to fill up and their dinner was served, and March tried to keep the conversation on a lighter note—not only for their sakes but for hers as well. She spoke of Melissa and Bill Brauner and of her own plans for the future. Mr. Hollister assured her that if she needed any further connections for jobs in New York City he would supply her with names in several of the financial firms downtown. "I'm sure any of them would be delighted with a young lady of your caliber," he said.

"Although it's hard to imagine that you could be satisfied living away from the islands," Mrs. Hollister put in, and her husband chided gently, "Now, Adele, when one is as young as Miss Raffin here, one welcomes the challenge of the new . . ."

March looked down at her plate, hoping that the sadness she was feeling was not written on her face for them to read. When she looked up, it was just in time to see Simon Wade entering the dining room with his daughter and Miranda Thompson. His eyes, moving around the room, met hers suddenly, and she could feel a moment's wild beating of her heart. Then at once, with a kind of cold deliberation, he looked away from her. They took a table across the room from where she sat with the Hollisters, but she could see them quite clearly. She was relieved to see that Simon's back was to her, but she had a good view of Miss Thompson, and thought that the woman's look was still disdainful. She had changed into a rather fussy, blue flowered dress that did not become her as well as the tailored suit she had worn earlier. The little girl Penny had changed for dinner into a simple white dress, sleeveless and with straight lines that accentuated her slender legginess and set off her rather exotic dark coloring. *She will be such a beauty in a few years*, March thought. *Will it be a blessing or will it cause trouble for her?*

Mrs. Hollister leaned toward her husband. "That's the little girl we were watching on the plane from Miami, William," she whispered. And to March she explained, "We couldn't help watching and listening, Miss Raffin. All the way over she kept up such a lively conversation with her mother—"

"She's a companion or governess, I believe," March said.

"Ah, perhaps that explains it," Mrs. Hollister said. "We had the decided impression the child was more than a match for the woman. Asking such probing questions, remember, William?"

Mr. Hollister nodded and grinned. "Such as why did the water change color as we flew nearer to the islands, how did the islands come to be there in the first place—I think the poor woman was at her wits' end to satisfy her curiosity."

March smiled and nodded as the conversation veered off on another tack and Mrs. Hollister began exclaiming over the pleasant qualities of Room Fifteen, which she insisted amiably was even pleasanter than Room Nine. But over and over March's eyes kept sliding across to the threesome at the table on the other side of the room. Conversation seemed to be largely between Simon and the little girl. Miss Thompson was drawn in now and then out of what March guessed was simple courtesy, but she had the impression that Miranda Thompson was quite content to be left to enjoy her meal. Considering her slender build, she was putting away an astonishingly hearty dinner. March suspected that the quality of Miss Emily's cooking might be a revelation to her, for several times she took second helpings. Even the dessert cart was rolled around twice for her selection.

Just as March and the Hollisters were getting up to leave, the three Massies and Ted Newburn entered the dining room. March carefully managed to keep her back turned to them. Somehow she dreaded meeting any of them at this moment. They caught sight of Simon at once and made for his table. There were exclamations from Monica and Caitlin, and Caitlin embraced the little girl. March recalled what Simon had told her, that the Massies were neighbors in Palm Beach, so of course they would all be acquainted. However, introductions appeared to be made in the case of Miranda Thompson, so apparently she had been hired only recently. The latest in a long succession of govenesses? March wondered.

She said her goodnights to the Hollisters in the lobby and headed for home. As she entered the little house and turned the light switch, she saw the living room flood with soft light, saw the bright island colors, the books, the pictures on the wall, and she knew with a sinking certainty that the Hollisters would love it. *It will all be settled by this time tomorrow*, March thought, *and my future as well*. And Simon Wade would be no more than a memory. It was a thought that should have provided comfort, but bitterly, March had to admit to herself that it did not.

The Hollisters were prompt in arriving the next morning, but March had been up early cleaning, straightening and dusting, cutting fresh flowers, making the house look its best. And when they entered and looked around and she saw the look of pleasure on Mrs. Hollister's face, the expression of approval on her husband's, she knew it was all a foregone conclusion.

"Young lady, I think you've made a sale," Mr. Hollister said after she had shown them through the house. "Suppose I call that lawyer in Johnsville and see if he can do the necessary paper work for us. Perhaps in a week or so we'll be able to go over there and have it all taken care of." Their faces were beaming, and Mrs. Hollister added quickly, "But no hurry, my dear, about your leaving. We don't want to rush you. Not at all. Please take all the time you want."

"It's all right," March said, forcing a smile. "The sooner the better. I'll show you around the boat when I come down to the marina a little later, although I guess you know it pretty well."

They chatted for a while and then said their goodbyes and March watched them go down the path talking happily together. Her own heart was even heavier than she had expected when she turned back into the house. She walked through the living room and into her father's room and stood for a long time looking out of his window toward the sea.

When she did at last make her way down to the inn she walked slowly, reluctantly, and her feet felt like lead weights. She scarcely paid attention to where she was going, and it was not until she was actually inside the lobby that she looked up in a startled way, realizing where she was, and in the next moment, that something was wrong. Paulie was talking on the telephone behind the desk and Simon was standing on the other side of the desk looking white-faced and anxious.

"Have you reached him?" he was asking. "Can he come right away?"

"Dr. Mercer?" Paulie was saying into the telephone. "Yes, it's Pauline Sanders at the Coral Cay Inn. Well—as I told your nurse, it's severe abdominal pains, temperature, nausea."

March approached the desk, but Simon did not see her. His attention was riveted on Paulie.

"During the night and still this morning," Paulie said. "Yes. Oh, we would appreciate it. Thank you, Doctor." She hung up and said to Simon, "He'll come at once."

"Good." His breath came out in a long sigh as if he had been holding it the whole time. He turned and hurried toward the stairs. "Thank you, Miss Sanders," he called over his shoulder.

Paulie turned and saw March. "What a morning!" she exclaimed.

"Is it the little girl?" March asked quickly. "Is it Penny?"

"No, it's that Miss Thompson. She was taken sick in the night. Dr. Mercer says he'll come as quickly as he can."

"I saw her at dinner. She was putting away a terrific amount of food."

"You saw that too?" Paulie said, and her eyebrows went up. "Even Miss Emily was curious. All very well for people to appreciate her cooking, she said, but that woman was overdoing it. Only I think it's more than simple indigestion. Mom's up there with her now, and she says she's really sick."

As they were talking, Simon returned holding Penny by the hand. Now he saw March at the desk, and his face, already grim-looking, stiffened into stoniness. He approached the desk and said, "Good morning, March. I don't believe you've met my daughter Penny. This is Miss Raffin, Penny."

"March," she said quickly, and took the small hand that was offered. "I'm so sorry to hear of your trouble," she said to Simon then.

"Yes. Poor Miss Thompson. I hope the doctor gets here soon." He turned away from her coolly, although Penny kept studying her with open curiosity. March was aware of her large brown eyes.

Simon addressed Paulie. "Miss Sanders, I'm taking Penny to the Massies' boat for the time being. They'll look after her while we wait for the doctor. I'll be back directly."

"Yes, of course. My mother will stay with Miss Thompson. Please don't worry about that, Mr. Wade," Paulie assured him.

"Are you staying here at the inn?" Penny asked March in the curious frank way of children.

"No, I live here on Coral Cay."

"All the time?" The little girl seemed astounded.

"Well, yes, all the time." It did not seem appropriate to explain at this moment that she would soon be leaving.

"Do you have your own house?"

"Yes."

"Gee." It was an expression of open wonderment, but before she could ask more questions her father seized her hand and said, "Come on, Penny. I'll leave you with the Massies for a while until I have a chance to talk with the doctor."

"I do hope everything's all right," March said.

"Thank you," he replied curtly, and turned away from the desk with the little girl. She called over her shoulder, "See you later, March!" and March lifted a hand and waved, but all she could see of Simon was a straight back turned stiffly toward her.

"Appendicitis," Don Sanders said in a low voice to the two girls. March had stayed on behind the desk to help Paulie sort mail, hand out keys, sell postcards and stamps, and tend the telephone. Both Don and

Marian Sanders were anxiously conferring with Dr. Mercer, who had hurried over at once from Coral Island, and who was now busily issuing orders for ice packs and blankets, and preparing to move Miranda Thompson in his own station wagon to a small private hospital on the larger island. Simon Wade himself had carried her carefully downstairs and placed her in the station wagon, where a makeshift bed had been arranged. March could hear him reassuring her. "Please don't worry, Miss Thompson. You'll be all right. I'll take care of everything. Just concentrate on getting well—you're in very good hands." Seeing him carry the sick woman so lightly and easily, March could not help remembering the feeling of those arms around her, could not help imagining the strength and security she would feel if they were carrying her. A wave of longing swept over her, the very feeling she had been trying to put behind her ever since the night of the party on the yacht.

As the station wagon pulled away, heading for the causeway road, another thought came to her. He'll have no one now to help him with Penny. And in spite of her own bitterness, in spite of the fact that she knew their relationship to be finished, she could not help feeling warmth toward the little girl, who had looked at her with such an open stare earlier. Could she possibly offer to help entertain Penny, or would it just reestablish something between Simon and her— the last thing in the world that she wanted? What if she were to keep a safe distance—not see him at all but only Penny. Could it do any harm?

"Back in a minute, Paulie," she said, and moved tentatively toward the veranda where Simon was still standing, talking with Don and Marian.

"Just the worst possible back luck, Mr. Wade," Marian was saying. Don Sanders put in, "However, you can be assured she'll receive top-notch medical care. Dr. Mercer's extremely capable." March could hear Simon's murmured reply, "I certainly am grateful to you both for handling it so well." Then Marian's voice again, "Of course you feel a responsibility, Mr. Wade, but really, you'll see, by tomorrow you'll be getting a good report on her and there'll be nothing more to worry about."

March put her hand on the door, ready to open it, feeling her heart pound wildly, when she was stopped by the sight of Caitlin and Penny coming up the walk from the marina. Caitlin was in her brief white bikini with a gauzy short beach coat thrown over it and swinging open with every step.

"Simon darling, what absolutely rotten luck," she sang out. "But not to worry. Just go ahead and do whatever you have to. I'll be happy to take care of Penny. We have a whole lot of good stuff planned to do, don't we, hon?" She swung the little girl's hand and Penny gave an enthusiastic hop and ran to her father.

"Caitlin wants us to rent bikes and explore the island. Can we do that, Daddy?"

Simon reached down to put his arm around her shoulders. "Sure, honey. That's very good of Caitlin. You and I are going to have some good times, too. I want to rent a boat and take you sight-seeing, and I want to show you my island, too, Whispering Pines. Only today I have to meet with a government man over in Johnsville. It'll give me a chance to stop in at the hospital too and inquire after Miss Thompson." He looked at Caitlin over the child's head. "I'd certainly be grateful, Caty."

Caitlin had come up the steps to stand beside him as Marian and Don headed toward the door. March shrank back so that she could not be seen in the dimness of the lobby, but she saw Caitlin seize Simon's free arm and press her golden-tan body against him. "You know I love doing things for you, Simon."

154

March turned and fled back to the desk as Marian and Don Sanders came in. Paulie took one look at her face and said, "What's up?"

"Caitlin Massie's taking over the job of governess, so it would appear."

Paulie gave a whoop of laughter which she silenced quickly with one hand. "Her nibs?" she whispered then. "Not exactly the type, would you say? She's figured out how to get next to him, though."

"Through Penny?"

"Well, he adores his daughter. It's written all over him. I guess anyone who'd make a fuss over Penny would rate pretty high with him."

"Yes." March was ashamed now to admit that she had had the same idea. Only not because of Simon, she told herself. In spite of him rather. Perhaps because of something she had seen in the little girl's face which showed through all the bounciness and exuberance. A trace, a shade, a faint suggestion deep in those brown eyes, of loneliness. She could see Paulie giving her a searching look and anticipated a question. Warding it off, she said quickly, "Seen the Hollisters, Paulie? I promised to show them the boat."

"I think I heard them say they were going walking along the beach. How did they like your house?"

"They're taking it," March said, and turned away hastily. Paulie had known her too long and too well not to be able to read her emotions with fair accuracy. And right now her emotions were the last things she wanted to discuss with anyone.

She found the Hollisters and showed them the boat, then took them out for a long ride and let Mr. Hollister handle the wheel for a time. It would be a challenge, he had said, looking pleased.

"Only you must be very careful about not attempting too much at first," March cautioned. "Let Tommy Monday advise you. And be sure to wear your life preservers always. I know the *Flower* will be in good hands with you," she said, managing with an effort to keep her voice steady.

By the time she returned to the inn she found Paulie sitting alone in the kitchen with her shoes off, drinking lemonade.

"This has *really* been a day!" she groaned. "I'm absolutely beat. Have some lemonade."

March sat down at the table with her and accepted the glass of lemonade Paulie poured from a frosty pitcher. "Where's Miss Emily?"

"Gone to the fishing boat. Wanted to make her own selection today. Or maybe she just took pity on me."

"I should be getting home," March said, but even as she said it she felt a reluctance to do so. Something about the little house had changed for her, in spite of its comfortable familiarity. *It's not mine anymore*, she thought. *Oh, actually it is, for another week or so, but in spirit I've already given it up.*

"Any news of the patient—or anyone?" she asked.

Paulie shook her head. "Simon Wade's not back yet. He'll have news, I'm sure." She took another sip of lemonade and set her glass down. "March, I wanted to ask you this morning, but everything got so hectic. Tommy told me what happened at the party the other night. He heard Ted Newburn and Simon Wade talking about it the day he took them to the Pines. March, you said you didn't care anything about him, but the way it sounded to me . . . "

The door opened and Marian Sanders stuck her head in, looking concerned, glasses dangling from their chain. "Girls, have you seen anything of those two?"

"What two?" Paulie asked.

"That Miss Massie and the little girl. They rented bikes from us and went off somewhere, but that was three hours ago. And it's a terribly hot day. Where could they have gotten to? I don't think that girl knows how fierce our island sun can be at this time of day. I warned them when they left but I thought Miss Massie was very casual about it.''

March and Paulie exchanged a look. "If they've gone up toward one of the high open areas where there's no shelter . . . '' March said.

"And some of the pathways are terribly rough and narrow, even for experienced bikers,'' Paulie added.

"Penny certainly can't be experienced, and I doubt if Caitlin Massie is either.''

March stood up. "I was about to start home, Aunt Marian,'' she said. "I'll look along the way and perhaps head up the path a bit and see if there's any sign of them.''

"Oh March, would you? And send them straight back if you find them.''

March waved her assent, already starting out the door. Paulie's voice followed her. "Come back for dinner, won't you.''

"Okay!'' She called it back over her shoulder, but the prospect made her gloomy. Paulie would be full of questions, she knew. Well, perhaps that was good, she shrugged to herself. Perhaps it was time she talked about her feelings with someone. Right now she was more concerned about little Penny Wade anyway than about her own troubles. Her heart was beginning to pound anxiously as she hurried up the wooded path.

She found the two of them walking their bikes gingerly down from the direction of the church clearing. Of the two, Caitlin looked in worse condition. Her fair complexion was beet-red. Her hair, pulled loose from its long braid, straggled around her face in wisps and tangles, and there were twigs stuck in it. An angry scratch was across one cheek. Her T-shirt was soaked with perspiration. Penny was plodding along sturdily, but March could see that her legs were covered with scratches and insect bites and her

157

face was pale with fatigue. Her eyes looked enormous.

"What happened to you two?" March demanded, hurrying up to them.

"We got lost," Caitlin moaned. "I mean, absolutely *lost*. I don't know how we ever did find our way back."

"I found it," Penny said with pride. "I remembered the landmarks."

"Good for you," March said.

"Hey, did you know there's something that looks like a church up there?"

"Yes, I knew. And it is a church. Look, leave the bikes here. You'd better come up to my house, both of you. You can rest a minute and wash up. Then you won't look so awful when you get back to the inn."

"Oh, my head!" Caitlin was still moaning. "That sun! We just couldn't get away from it!"

"Midday on this island is a poor time for biking," March said, but even toward Caitlin she could not feel gloating—the girl's misery was so complete. "Come on. It's only a short way from here."

She led the way up the path to her own house, and when they had stepped inside its cool dimness, all the blinds drawn and the great fig tree spreading its shade overhead, Caitlin collapsed on the couch with a groan. But Penny stood in the middle of the room looking around—just the way Simon had stood, March thought.

"Is this your house?"

"Yes."

"Doesn't anybody live here with you?"

"No, not any more. Come along, I'll get you both a drink."

Caitlin groaned and refused to budge, so March brought the drink of cool water to her. Penny, after she had had a drink, walked through the rooms in a wondering way, reaching out to touch things, looking, examining.

Caitlin at last stirred and asked where she might wash up, and March directed her to the bathroom. She took Penny into the kitchen with her while she brought a washcloth, cotton and disinfectant and went to work on her scratched legs and the red itching insect bites. Then she brushed the little girl's short dark curls, getting rid of the grass, twigs, and dust, and making them shine again.

"There now. I don't think your father will be too alarmed when he sees you."

"How do you know my daddy?" Penny asked suddenly.

"Oh, I happened to meet him," March answered vaguely. She turned away, fussing with cotton and the disinfectant bottle. To herself she thought, *no matter what he thinks of me, I must speak to him. Caitlin is a dangerous companion for Penny. She's irresponsible, she doesn't know the island, and more, she has no moral strength to offer Penny, no strong firm guidance in right and wrong. The very strength every child needs so desperately.*

Caitlin's appearance as she rejoined them only reinforced her thinking. She had washed her face and rebraided her hair, brushed off her clothing, and, refreshed, she looked altogether casual and offhand, as if the whole affair had been no more than an exciting escapade.

"Guess we'd better be starting back, hon," she said airily. As if it were an afterthought she added, "Thanks, March." The whole affair was behind her, and even the recent incident of the records was gone from her mind. March's help she accepted as no more than her due. Angrily March thought that she would certainly have to speak to Simon. Then at the door Penny seized her hand and said, "I guess maybe it would be better if we didn't tell Daddy – about getting lost, I mean—okay, March? You know, he worries about me sometimes, even though it's dumb."

March hesitated. "Perhaps not. We'll see." But she would not promise. The whole incident had serious overtones, and she was not at all sure that it would be wise to keep it from Simon, even though she dreaded speaking to him for fear of revealing her own emotions.

After they had left she went back inside and took a long, slow shower. Then she picked up the soiled towels tossed down by Caitlin, and dressed casually in white slacks, a navy top, and sandals. The sun was low, all the shadows long, the air heavy with fragrance as she walked back down to the inn. She avoided the kitchen door this time, since she knew Miss Emily would be busy with dinner preparations. Instead she went around to the front door and looked in at the lobby to where Paulie was once more at the desk.

"Be ready in a couple of minutes, March," Paulie sang out, and March answered, "I'll wait for you out here." She took a chair on the cool veranda, now largely deserted as guests made their way indoors in ones and twos toward the dining room. At the marina, fishing boats were returning with their loads of tourists. Stan Massie was probably on one of them, March thought with amusement, and wondered whether his luck was holding.

Suddenly she heard the front door open and close and Simon came out. She looked away quickly, but then in the next moment thought, *whatever is the matter with me? At least I can act like an adult, I hope.* But it was hard, seeing him standing there so suntanned and tall. He was casually dressed for dinner in navy slacks and a soft cream-colored shirt open at the neck. He caught sight of her sitting there and his mouth quirked grimly.

"Oh. Hello," he said curtly, but he did not smile.

"Hello." She tried to be equally cool. "How is Miss Thompson?"

160

"Doing well, thank you. Operated on early this afternoon and everything's fine."

"I'm so glad. Isn't your daughter with you?"

"She's napping. She came in and fell asleep, I gather, after her bike ride."

March hesitated, weighing her decision about speaking to him, if only for Penny's safety.

"I've been wondering," she said tentatively, "if you think Caitlin is the best possible companion for Penny."

He turned to look at her squarely, and his mouth took on a one-sided smile that had a cool, sardonic look. "Is that any of your business?" he said coldly.

March blushed. She felt rebuffed and ashamed at having put herself in such a position. "I only wondered," she said hesitantly. "Caitlin isn't well acquainted with the island, and her judgment might not be . . . " She broke off, uncertain as to how to continue.

Someone was coming up the walk toward the inn. March turned and saw Caitlin, dressed for dinner in a pale pink silk dress, her long hair loose around her shoulders, her diamond earrings winking in the late golden sunlight. Simon turned and saw her at the same time.

"Caitlin! I was just coming to pick you up."

"Simon, love, I was too famished to wait. You don't mind moving our dinner date up a little, do you? I think it must have been all that outdoor exercise." Her eyes went to March and she lifted a hand in casual greeting. March wondered if it was only her imagination or if there was moment's uneasiness in those eyes. But at once Caitlin gave all her attention to Simon, putting a hand lightly on his arm and tilting her head up to kiss him lightly. He frowned at the scratch still visible on her cheek.

"What happened to you?"

"Nothing worth mentioning. A twig caught me as we were biking today. Where's Penny?"

"Still sleeping. I'm just going up to wake her for dinner."

"Oh. You don't think you ought to let her sleep?" It was blatantly obvious to March that she would prefer Simon's company without Penny.

"No, she'd never sleep tonight then. I'll go get her. Won't be a minute."

"Let me come along. Maybe I can help her dress."

"What would I do without you, Caty?"

Neither of them looked toward March again as they went in.

CHAPTER 10

SHE MET TOMMY MONDAY on the dock two days later. "March! Where have you been keeping yourself?"

"Oh, just busy, Tommy. Lots of business to take care of."

His big grin faded. "Yeh. I heard you're selling your house. Gee, it's going to seem funny without you on Coral Cay. Well look, we never did have our date. Why don't you and Paulie and I have a picnic on the beach tonight?"

"Oh, that sounds wonderful," she said. There was a time, she knew, when he would have wanted to be alone with her, but ever since her return from New York she had sensed a different attitude in him. There was distance between them now, as if he knew, just as she did, that the old days, the old relationships were gone forever. She knew he had always been fond of Paulie. Was it perhaps turning into something more serious? She was happy at what she sensed was developing between them, yet it gave her a lonely feeling too, a sense of loss. *They belong here but I don't*, she thought. *Not any more.*

After she had said goodbye to him she made her way home, but once there she did not set herself to any of the tasks she knew she should be doing. Instead she went into the captain's room and looked around her. Everything was neatly sorted, stacked, packed in boxes, yet she had still not been able to take the decisive step of giving anything away. She went to the window where the telescope stood and ran her hand lovingly along its smooth length. It stood where it always had—looking out toward sea. March leaned over and looked through it, out toward the blue water, the shoreline, on up to the bright horizon. She moved it a little to the right and focused on the reef where she and Simon Wade had gone snorkeling. It seemed light-years ago now. Suddenly she came to attention. For a long moment she watched, her whole body growing rigid. Then with a little cry she turned and ran from the house, down the sloping path, past the inn without a pause, on out to the dock where the *Flower of the Sea* bobbed gently at its berth.

Without hesitation she leaped down onto the boat and began ripping off the canvas cover, not worrying about neatness, tossing it in a heap on the floor of the boat, then untying bow and stern lines and starting up the motor. She heard feet pounding on the dock and saw Paulie running after her.

"March, I saw you go tearing past. What is it?"

"Caitlin Massie's out there on the reef with Penny."

"I know. They've been renting that small boat of Tommy's. It's not a hard one to manage. A kid could do it."

"That's not the point. I think they're snorkeling." She was already starting to push away from the dock.

"They can't get into too much trouble," Paulie protested.

Over her shoulder March exploded, "But don't you bet she's wearing those precious earrings of hers?"

"The diamonds? Good grief, March, if she loses them she won't even miss them! Oh gosh—I see what you mean." But March did not hear any more. She was busy navigating the *Flower* out of the shelter of the marina and into open water as fast as she could. A fishtail of white foam arched up behind the boat as she pushed the throttle forward and sped out toward the reef.

She pulled up close to the small rented boat and hurriedly cut the motor. Caitlin and Penny, sensing the commotion, both came to the surface and lifted their masks. Cupping both hands to her mouth March shouted, "Penny! Caitlin! Come on out. Get in your boat!"

Both of them obeyed the imperative tone in her voice and climbed into their boat. They stared at her in bewilderment as March took a deep breath and let it out with relief. The two girls were using a second boat owned by Tommy Monday and frequently rented to tourists—a twenty-five foot runabout ideal for snorkeling or water skiing. March knew that Stan Massie was renting it by the week to keep Caitlin amused.

"What's going on?" Caitlin demanded angrily.

"Hi, March," Penny said affably. "Want to come snorkeling with us? You should see the fish down there!"

"No, Penny, and you'd better come back to the marina now."

"Well, I am getting sorta tired," Penny admitted. "You know, that's hard work, snorkeling? You get real beat."

"You do," March agreed. Over Penny's head she said sternly to Caitlin, "That's why an experienced snorkeler always swims upwind of his boat, not downwind the way you were doing. If you get tired it can be next to impossible to make it back to the boat against wind and current."

Caitlin's face took on an ugly look of resentment.

"Big deal," she muttered. "Thanks a lot, Goody Two-Shoes. Any other advice?"

March felt anger surging through her so furiously that she was for the moment grateful she was in another boat. If she had been near enough she would have grabbed Caitlin and shaken her.

"Yes, just one small matter. Those diamonds in your ears. Any fool knows enough not to wear anything shiny underwater around here. A perfect attention-getter for barracudas. And sharks."

She saw Penny's eyes go wide with disbelief, and Caitlin's face turn ashy-pale under its golden tan.

"They don't advertise *that* in the travel brochures," she snapped.

"It's not a common occurrence. But then, most people have sense enough to ask advice before doing something like this."

Caitlin turned her back and began angrily pulling up the anchor and then starting the boat. With a flourish she took off, leaving March in a rocking swell. Distantly March could see Penny's small figure waving to her.

Back on land, March paused at the inn only long enough to reassure Paulie that everything was all right, then plodded homeward. She was hot, tired and angry. No matter how she tried to avoid it, everything that happened to her seemed to remind her of Simon just when she most wanted to put him out of her mind. Caitlin Massie's cool insolence was the final abrasive touch. Not a word of thanks, not the smallest hint of friendliness had escaped her. *Not that I want her friendship*, March thought angrily.

She banged into the house and slammed the door behind her, turned on a cool shower and stood under it for a long time. She then dried off and considerably soothed, slipped into a cool white cotton dressing gown, tied loosely at the waist with a sash. She lay down on the bed and was almost instantly asleep.

She awoke to the dark golden light of later afternoon and to an insistent pounding on her front door. Barefooted and sleepy, pulling the dressing gown around her, she went to answer it. Penny Wade was standing on the doorstep. Her dark curls were still slightly damp. She had changed into shorts and a T-shirt. She was already growing rosily tan, March noticed, her cheekbones dusted with sunburn.

"Hi, March. I looked for you on the dock but I guess I missed you."

"I came straight home," March said. "Come on in, Penny."

The little girl stepped inside. "Boy, you sure were mad as hell out there in the boat," she said.

March's eyebrows lifted slightly. "Does your father like you to use language like that?"

"Oh, I don't use it around him," the girl said, flopping down on March's couch. "Only it drives Miss Thompson up the wall. I do it sometimes to bug her."

"That isn't really fair, is it?" March asked, sitting down beside her, and Penny shrugged. "Has Miss Thompson been with you long?"

"No, only a few months. I get rid of governesses pretty fast," Penny admitted with some pride. "I don't think this one will come back, even after she's well. I've been to three private schools already too."

"Your father must worry about you."

"No, he doesn't worry about me," the little girl said, and her small face took on a look of distance. "I don't even see him too much."

"Well, of course he must be very busy. And I suppose he travels a lot," March said.

"Yeah. I've got this aunt I stay with sometimes—only she gets married a lot. And when she's on a honeymoon or getting a divorce or stuff like that I have to stay with a governess." Penny looked at her curiously. "How come you came tearing out after us that way?"

"I saw you from my window here and I saw the direction the wind was coming from. I just thought it wasn't wise, what you and Caitlin were doing."

"Yeah, well, Caitlin doesn't know too much about it, I guess." She paused. "How come you know? I mean, all that about the wind and everything?"

"Someone taught me."

"Oh." Penny walked to the window and looked out. "You can't see from here," she said accusingly. "You can't even see the water."

"Not here, the window in the other room. And I was looking through a telescope. Here. I'll show you." March got up and led the way into her father's room, showed the little girl the telescope and how to look through it. "There. See how well you can make out the reef?"

"Wow. That's great." She looked through it for a long time before finally tearing herself away and following March back to the living room.

"How about a cookie?" March asked. "And a glass of milk?"

"Okay." Penny followed her into the kitchen. "Who was it that taught you all that stuff about the currents and the barracudas and all that?" she asked with a frown.

"My father," March answered. She poured milk and set cookies on the table. Penny sat down and curled her feet around the chair legs.

"Is he away someplace?"

"He's dead."

"Oh." The girl paused. Then she asked, "Is that telescope his? And that room?"

"Yes."

"Did he used to live here with you?"

"Yes."

"Don't you have a mother?"

"My mother died when I was very little."

Penny lifted large brown eyes to March's. "So did

168

mine." She took a bite of cookie and drank some of the milk, leaving a rim of white on her upper lip. After a moment she lowered her eyes and asked, "Don't you get lonesome sometimes?"

"Yes, of course, now and then. But when I do, I think of how he has gone to an eternal life with Jesus."

"What's eternal?"

"It means for always."

"Oh." There was a pause. "I know about Jesus."

"You do?"

"Well, some. You know. Christmas and stuff. I know about the Baby Jesus in the manger."

Something squeezed painfully around March's heart as she thought she detected a longing, a hunger in the little girl's voice. Something wistful was hiding there. *But it's not up to me*, March thought. *Simon is the one who . . .*

"Hey!" Penny said suddenly. "Was that your church? That one we saw up on top of the hill?"

March nodded and sank down into a chair across the table from her, smiling a little as she watched the cookies being demolished. When the plate held only crumbs and the milk had disappeared, there was another knock at the door.

"Hey, I'll get it, shall I?" Penny said, and before March could answer, skipped out of the kitchen and over to the front door. "Hi, Daddy," March heard her say, and March's heart turned over with a thump. She got up and walked toward the living room, trying hard to adjust her expression to one of indifference before she entered.

He stood in the doorway framed against the sunlight, looking at her. The light was behind him so that she could not read his expression clearly, but she could feel his eyes on her as she stood there in the thin cotton dressing gown, her cheeks still flushed from her nap, her hair tousled around her shoulders. Penny seized his hand and pulled him inside.

"March has been showing me her father's telescope," Penny chattered on. "Do you know you can see way out in the water with it—as far as the reef? That's how come she saw . . . " The little girl paused, realizing she was trapping herself as she saw his look turn into a reprimand.

"I heard about the business on the reef," he said severely, and looked up at March. "Hello, March." He said it stiffly, and his expression had a tight controlled look, emotion held in check. "Your friend Pauline told me just now what happened. I'm very grateful to you for thinking and acting so quickly."

She thought it was costing him an effort to unbend toward her. His voice had lost its arrogant brittleness; he seemed to be making an effort at sincerity. *If* such a thing were possible with Simon Wade, she reminded herself, and answered, "Luckily Penny was in no danger. It's just that the potential was there."

Their eyes met over the little girl's head as both of them remembered the day they had themselves been lost in the underwater magic of the reef.

"Still, I'm very grateful," he said, "I'm sure Caitlin meant no harm, but she's inexperienced."

In some things, March thought bitterly. *Totally capable when it comes to men, though.* "It's quite all right," she said.

"It was her father's telescope," Penny went on, blithely unaware of the currents of attraction and animosity flowing between the two adults. "He used to live in this house with her. She went to a church up on the hill. I saw it." It seemed to March that something wistful had crept into the little girl's voice.

"Penny, perhaps that's something March doesn't care to discuss," he said.

"Of course I want to," March said quickly. "Why wouldn't I?"

"I only thought the subject might be painful."

"Memories of my father are the least painful part of

170

my life," she said almost defiantly. "Everything that's been good in my life—all the best things—I got from him."

"I see," he said. "Then you've been very fortunate." He turned to his daughter. "All right, you. Run along down to the inn now. I'll be right behind you. You're going to need a head start to get cleaned up and changed for dinner."

"Okay, Daddy. See you, March," she sang out, and slipped through the door. He stood there uncertainly for a moment and March, determined not to make anything easier for him, stood in stony silence.

"Penny seems quite taken with you," he said at last, sounding a little stiff.

"She's a very winning little girl," March answered with equal stiffness.

"A handful sometimes," he said with a shake of his head. "This business of poor Miss Thompson has certainly complicated everything."

"I don't believe Miss Thompson's illness is the real problem," March said impulsively, and then at once wished she had not said it. But somehow she felt that Penny's future was in the balance, that there were things that had to be brought into the open.

"What do you mean by that?" he frowned.

"I mean that Penny is able to dispose of governesses pretty fast. Isn't that so?"

He looked uncomfortable. "I'll admit it's difficult nowadays to find well qualified people."

"And of course you're much too busy. I mean, to take a hand in your daughter's upbringing."

A chill crept into his voice. "I do have the small matter of making a living to take care of. I spend as much time with Penny as I'm able to."

"Yes, I see how you manage to work her in between more important matters."

His face turned dark with anger. "Now look here, that's uncalled-for! It happens that my work takes me all over the world. I'm sorry, but that's the way it is."

"Then why don't you take Penny with you?"

"But she's a little girl! She can't be snatched out of school and trotted off to Italy or Greece or Morocco just on a whim."

"She's been snatched out of three private schools already, hasn't she? Not bad for a seven-year-old."

"Now just a minute."

"No, you wait a minute," March said firmly. "There's an education in seeing Greece and Italy and Morocco too, isn't there? And the important thing would be that she'd be with you. She needs you. She needs your strength and love and yes, your discipline too. Maybe at seven it doesn't look too important, but I can promise you it will become very important in a few years."

"Look here, you've seen Penny. Does she seem like a problem to you? You said yourself she's winning, likeable. Why are you blowing this all out of proportion?"

"I have seen her, and I agree. She's a darling child. But she's also on vacation, free as a bird and having a wonderful time here, especially in the absence of any supervision. Why wouldn't she be on her best behavior? It isn't always quite so smooth though, is it?"

She saw a flush of color sweep across his lean face, and knew she had struck close to an uncomfortable truth.

"I don't know how I managed to get along without you to run my life for me," he said with cold sarcasm.

"I don't want to run your life," she flared, "but I know that every child's life needs a strong center, something to hang onto. And you haven't given Penny that."

"You don't know anything about it!"

"Maybe you need something too," she said quietly. "Something to give meaning to your own life."

"I have my work . . . "

"I'm talking about God's love," March said simply.

172

"I'm talking about acceptance of Christ, of coming to Him and letting Him change your life." She saw the flush in his face deepen and for a moment a deep stillness lay between them. Then bitterness altered his expression, and he said, "This is really my own affair. I only came here to express my thanks to you, but you seem to have turned it into an attack on me."

"If anything's attacking you, it should be your conscience," March said crisply, her patience wearing thin. "And believe it or not, I don't want any part of your problems. If you could manage to stay away from me from now on, I'd be grateful."

"That shouldn't be hard to do," he snapped, striding out.

March tried to stay cheerful that night as she picnicked on the beach with Tommy and Paulie. The three of them laughed together, remembering old times, pranks, and escapades at school. They swam by moonlight, ate their lunch hungrily, sat by the fire to warm up, and at last walked back barefooted along the sandy strip. March, slightly removed from the other two, noticed how close together they stayed. Her own loneliness stabbed at her.

Tommy looked up at the great bowl of the sky with its glittering canopy of stars. "I think the weather's going to change," he said, and sniffed the air.

Later as she lay in bed listening to the murmur of the wind in the fig tree outside her open window, feeling the stir of the night air and smelling its sweetness, March turned her face to her pillow and sobbed, seeing behind her closed eyelids the dark anger of Simon's face as he left her earlier, feeling the touch of his lips on hers as they had seemed to envelop her whole body, her whole being, that afternoon on the reef. She had put an end now to anything he might have felt for her. It was truly over. Indeed, it had never really been. All of it had been a dream of her own creation. And now even the dream

173

was gone. Lying there quietly in the dark, she tried to tell herself it was all for the best, but it was a long time before her heart stopped its restless aching, and only toward dawn did she fall into an uneasy sleep.

Tommy's prediction of a change in the weather did not seem accurate, March noted as she got up the next morning to bright sunshine. She was feeling weary, not at all rested. There was a heaviness in her movements a slow dragging lethargy about everything she did. The Hollisters had told her the evening before that the appointment with the lawyer in Johnsville had been made. It was only three days away. It could not be too soon for her, she thought. Once that was settled, a great load would be lifted from her shoulders. All that would be left to do would be to pack her suitcases and make reservations for her return flight to New York. Until then there seemed to be no purpose to her days, no reason to get up at all.

She stood in her nightgown at her window and gave herself a brisk shake, like a dog coming out of the water, she thought, trying to smile at her own misery. *Well, if there's nothing of my own that needs doing,* she told herself sternly, *at least I can pitch in and help at the inn. No use sitting around here wallowing in self-pity.* There was no reason to avoid the inn where she had always come and gone so casually. No reason except that she might encounter Simon there. But after their last conversation it seemed unlikely that they would have trouble avoiding each other. No doubt he did not want to see her any more than she wanted to see him. And Paulie and her parents had been putting in long hours. Between the beginning of the seasonal tourist trade—the honeymooners, the group tours, the repeating guests—and then all the upheaval occasioned by Miss Thompson's illness and the Massies with extra guests to be put up, the Sanders family had really been working overtime. It would do her good to keep busy.

She showered and dressed for work in comfortable slacks, red-and-white checkered shirt and deck shoes. Then after a quick bowl of cereal and a glass of juice she walked at a brisk pace down the sloping path to the inn, trying deliberately to put herself into a better frame of mind.

She found Paulie having her own hasty breakfast in the kitchen. "Mom's at the desk," Paulie explained between bites of toast, "but I have to hurry and relieve her. She's going in to Johnsville to call on Miss Thompson. Ed Beaslie's taking her in his taxi. She thinks it's her duty, I guess, and she wants to go early. There's a storm due later in the day."

"Is there? I didn't have my radio on. Anyway, I thought you might need some help today. Put me to work, will you? I want to keep busy."

Paulie gave her a probing look but did not comment. "Okay. There's certainly plenty to do around here. Maybe Miss Emily could use some help too."

"Only help I need is for everybody to get out of my way," Miss Emily grumbled. She was packing a hamper with sandwiches, hard-boiled eggs and fruit.

"Who's having a picnic?" March asked.

"Not a picnic. It's for that Mr. Wade. He and Tommy going to Whispering Pines."

"Oh." March tried hard to stay offhand. "They certainly didn't pick a very good day for it if there's a storm coming."

"Oh, they'll be back long before it hits," Paulie said. "Tommy knows all about things like that."

March gave her friend an affectionate glance as she heard the pride in her voice.

"Yes, of course. I just meant that Simon Wade could have waited for a good day. It wouldn't hurt him to be a bit more considerate."

"I *like* him," Miss Emily said crossly. "I like a man who appreciates good food." She slapped down the lid of the hamper with the air of having had the last word on the subject. March and Paulie exchanged a look, and March said, "All right, where do I start?"

Paulie pushed her chair back from the table. "Well, Tiny's nieces are working upstairs in the rooms, and Tiny's going to be busy clearing in the dining room and then setting up tables for the lunch hour. How about the lobby? Would you mind a bit of vacuuming and dusting?"

"You're the boss," March said. Since informality and family management were trademarks of the inn, Paulie's request seemed a perfectly normal one to her. Indeed, there were even longtime guests such as the Hollisters who had more than once been known to do their own bed-making and room-straightening. Paulie helped her wrestle the large commercial-style vacuum cleaner out of the utility closet and drag it into the lobby, where she at once set about energetically vacuuming while Paulie took over from her mother behind the desk. As she worked, dragging the noisy cleaner around after her on its stubborn wheels, March began to feel the frustrations and irritations of the past week growing lighter, and she herself began to feel, if not completely happy, at least more in control of herself. Concentrating on her work and with the roar of the cleaner in her ears, she did not notice that Simon had come downstairs to the lobby, nor did she hear his voice as he used the desk telephone. Only when she had turned off the switch and pulled out her dustrag to start polishing furniture did she become aware of it. She felt a sudden tension, a rush of emotional trembling, and kept her back turned to him.

"Ed? How's it going there?" she heard him say. "You did? Good. I'm glad it's settled. And what about Harris in Pittsburgh? Did you talk to him? Does it fit in with his time schedule? Good, because things are moving along here. I think we'll get the approval in a matter of days. Will you be ready at your end then? Sounds great. Listen, have you talked to Diana? How's she doing? She is! Can't you talk her out of it? Well, we'll cross that bridge when we come to it . . . ''

March went back in memory to the plane trip from New York, seeing again the beautiful Diana with her alabaster face and dark coiled hair. She recalled how the woman had clung to Simon when he put her into a taxi at the airport, and the words overheard, pleading, *Won't I be seeing you again soon?* An affair that Simon had thought over and done with, obviously. Now it sounded as if he might have been wrong. And what was it that she could not be talked out of— pursuing him here to Coral Cay, perhaps?

She heard him hang up the telephone and she edged her way into a corner, hoping to stay out of sight, but a moment later Penny came bouncing down the stairs and caught sight of her.

"Hi, March!" she called out cheerfully, and March had to look up. "Hi, Penny," she replied and then, unavoidably, met his glance. He nodded, an icy look that put more distance between them than the space of the inn lobby. She saw that he was loaded down with the lunch hamper, a roll of blueprints like the ones she had seen him carrying the other day, a Polaroid camera and a notebook.

"Come along, Penny," he said curtly, and the little girl ran to accompany him out the front door. March guessed that she was to be left in Caitlin Massie's care again and hoped that Simon had spoken seriously to Caitlin about being more cautious and responsible.

She gave her own attention to her work once more and spent the rest of the morning helping out with whatever Paulie directed her to do, so that the time flew by more quickly than she would have imagined. She and Paulie had a late lunch together in a corner of the dining room and then Marian Sanders returned from her visit to Johnsville.

"Up and walking around, looking quite fit already,"

she said of Miss Thompson. "But quite anxious to go home to the states." So Penny's guess was correct, March thought, and now a new governess would have to be found.

By midafternoon it was clouding over and a wind was rising. Paulie's small radio behind the desk warned of a front that would be moving through by late afternoon—severe squalls and thunderstorms. Tommy Monday and Simon returned from Whispering Pines and Paulie hurried out to speak to Tommy on the veranda, while March tried to look busy behind the desk. But Simon did not come in, and when Paulie returned she explained, "They're going over to Johnsville in Tommy's truck. Tommy had to pick up some machine parts and Simon Wade has some business there so he's hitching a ride with him. Tommy says the storm's due soon."

"I think I'd better go to the dock and see if my boat's secure," March said. Storms in April seldom lasted long, she knew, but often brought high winds and torrential downpours.

Clouds had begun to move in and the wind was rising as she walked to the marina and out along the dock toward her boat. She was surprised to see Ted Newburn there pacing up and down fretfully and looking anxious. He was wearing faded jeans and a windbreaker and his light hair was blowing around his forehead.

"Hello, March," he said. "How bad is this thing going to be? Can you tell?"

"Goodness no. Nobody ever seems to be able to tell. But you don't have anything to worry about," she reassured him teasingly. "The *Ayes of Texas* can certainly ride out any storm. Just relax and enjoy it. Storms are rather exciting around here."

"It's not the *Ayes of Texas* I'm worried about," Ted said. "It's Caitlin and Penny in that twenty-five-foot runabout they've been using all week."

An apprehensive chill swept over March. "You don't mean they've gone out in this . . ." She broke off incredulously as his face told her they had. "I can't believe Mr. Massie didn't stop them. He's an experienced boatman. He knows better than that. Why did he let them go?"

"He didn't. He and Monica haven't been here since yesterday. They're with some friends aboard a hundred-foot sailboat off Green Turtle. They're not due back till later tonight or tomorrow."

"But *you* should have stopped them then!"

"Well, even assuming I could ever stop Caitlin from doing anything, which is doubtful, I didn't see them until they were almost out of sight."

"When did they go? And which way?" March demanded.

"They headed out to meet Simon a half hour or so ago."

"To meet Simon!"

"Yes, he and Tommy went to that island of his."

"But they came back! Didn't you see them?" But then March realized they had made only a quick stop at the hotel and at once left in the truck. "Didn't Caitlin see Tommy's boat was back and tied to the dock where it always is?"

"Well, I suspect one boat looks pretty much like another to Caitlin. To me too, I'm afraid. I think it was Caitlin's idea to surprise Simon by showing up at that island on their own."

"But it must have been starting to cloud over and blow when they left. What's the matter with her?" March muttered angrily. She had already leaped onto her own boat and started to uncover it.

"I think she may have an idea the wind and weather will adjust themselves to her whims," Ted said ruefully. As he realized what March was doing, he said in sudden alarm, "Look here, is it really serious? I mean—I thought I was just being jittery."

"You have reason to be jittery," she said grimly. 'What are you going to do?"

"I'm going after them. Untie that stern line and jump in," she ordered curtly. "I'll need someone with me. If they're in trouble I won't be able to do everything alone." *If I'm lucky enough to find them in time*, she thought.

For a moment Ted hesitated and a sudden despair clutched at March's heart. *He won't be able to do it*, she thought. *He doesn't know bow from stern and he'll probably freeze just when I need him*. But in the next instant he came to life. He hurried to unfasten the *Flower's* stern line and jumped in beside March. She was busily putting on a life preserver. She tossed another one to Ted.

"Here," she said. "Put this on. We may both need them before we're though."

CHAPTER 11

EVEN THE PROTECTED WATER of the marina had a small chop to it as they started out toward open water. March had not bothered to put up the Bimini top—it would just be in the way, and a nuisance in the wind. While Ted struggled with the fastenings of his life jacket she radioed the marina requesting a check.

"This is Coral Cay Marina," came the answer, unmistakably in Paulie's voice. Tommy and a few other experienced islanders took turns manning the transmitter, but Paulie was quite capable of taking over, as March knew.

"*Flower of the Sea* requesting a radio check," March said, and Paulie's voice crackled back at her, "I read you, *Flower of the Sea*. March is that you? Where on earth do you think you're going?"

March tried to keep her voice matter-of-fact. "Coral Cay Marina, I am headed around Rocky Point and northwesterly toward Whispering Pines."

"Get back to the marina at once, *Flower of the Sea*. A storm is due to hit full force within minutes." March did not reply, and Paulie demanded, "Do you read me, *Flower of the Sea*?"

"I read you, Coral Cay Marina. Paulie, I'm going after Caitlin and Penny. They're out there somewhere in the runabout."

Paulie's gasp was audible even over the noise of the engine and the rising wind. "March, you can't go after them alone. Come back in at once."

"Ted Newburn is with me, Paulie. We'll be all right. Over and out." March turned off the radio with a determined snap and gave her attention to her navigating. The sky had darkened noticeably since they started out, and the water that had been sparkling azure only moments before was now a menacing gray-green.

March gripped the wheel firmly and peered ahead toward Rocky Point, the wooded northeastern tip of Coral Cay. Beside her Ted stood in his clumsy life jacket, his hair blowing wildly, saying nothing, although March could see that his fingers, clamped to the top of the windshield, were white and rigid. Lightning split the sky and thunder roared after it. March swung the *Flower* to port and headed directly into a wind that was raging in from the northwest, although there was no rain with it as yet. They were in six-foot seas now and their progress was slow. March adjusted the speed of the boat so that the bow rose to meet each wave rather than being driven hard into it. Experienced though she was, she could not help being aware in the very pit of her stomach of the awesome power of the sea. It surrounded them, loomed over them, menaced them on every side.

"Keep your eyes open for their boat!" she shouted to Ted, and he nodded, but the only time they had a good view of the surrounding water was when they were at the top of a wave. When they plunged into the trough between waves all they could see was a wall of water. The wavering pole and faded rag marking the first reefs appeared to starboard. Both March and Ted peered anxiously toward the reefs, but there was no sign of the other boat. March was creeping forward as fast as she dared in the heavy seas.

"Do you think we could have missed them?" Ted shouted.

March shook her head even though she was not at all sure.

"There's more ahead!" she said, and inched forward. The second set of reefs marked the approach to Whispering Pines. For one desperate moment March thought of the broken ship she and Simon had inspected on the rocks of Solitude Point that day which now seemed years behind her. *Dream Come True* —she could still see the name on the fading hull. She tried to put all such thoughts out of her mind. She must concentrate. She must not let anything distract her. She squinted into the gloom, scanning the water.

"Ted! Over there!" she cried, pointing off the starboard bow. He followed the gesture. "That's it!" he shouted.

The small boat was bobbing like a cork in the huge waves. It was still in open water, but the reef lay only a short distance away. *Crouching and waiting*, March thought, and shivered. There was no sign of either Penny or Caitlin.

For the space of an instant March held her breath, trying to remember everything she knew of seamanship, of navigation, every trick, every technique the captain had taught her. Most of all she tried to remember his courage, his calmness—qualities that had never failed him, even in his last desperate illness. "Captain . . ." She breathed silently, and it almost seemed that he was there beside her, giving her courage. "Everything in moderation, nothing excessive," he had always told her. "Slowly, carefully. And always remember, my girl, you're never alone. In the roughest seas, Someone is watching over you. Someone cares." March closed her eyes and murmured a silent prayer, feeling strength flow back.

Then she swung the wheel to starboard, heading toward the smaller boat.

She made a slanting approach so that her own bow remained at an angle of forty-five degrees to the swells. She knew that the more headway was reduced in meeting heavy seas, the less would be the strain on the hull. Also, by going slowly she would avoid having the propeller race as each wave lifted it clear of the water, then vibrate wildly as it hit the water again.

Lightning flashed and thunder rolled menacingly. Ted leaned close to her. "Have you ever seen it this bad?"

She nodded. "Plenty of times," she shouted back reassuringly. Actually it was the truth. She had been in water like this often, and even now she would not be so frightened if she did not feel responsibility for the lives of Penny, Caitlin, and Ted. She knew the water, the depths, the uncharted obstructions, and she was confident of the seaworthiness of her boat. But a rescue under such conditions was something else again. Even with experienced help it would not have been easy, and Ted Newburn was anything but that. If only the rain would hold off!

As they drew nearer to the other boat she asked, "Can you tell if they're under power or stalled out?"

"Can't tell yet," Ted said. "I don't see anyone aboard." The *Flower* edged closer. "It's just drifting!" Ted cried. "The engine's not running but the anchor isn't out."

March was as close as she dared venture now. She began making wide slow circles around the drifting boat. Lightning kept cutting through the black skies and the temperature was dropping. Both of them were drenched with ocean spray but March felt anything but cold, and she could tell that Ted had not even noticed it, even though his jeans and windbreaker were soaked. He cupped his hands to his mouth and began shouting in the direction of the other boat.

"Caitlin, are you all right? Caitlin! Penny! Answer me!"

There was no response. March, trying hard to concentrate on her navigating, felt her heart sink as she kept remembering Penny standing at her door, long-legged in her khaki shorts. *Hi, March, I looked for you on the dock.* She shook her head, trying to clear away the strands of hair that blew in front of her eyes.

"We have to do something," she told Ted. "The wind's blowing us toward the reefs."

Just then the *Flower* crested a huge wave and slammed into a trough. Ted lost his balance and went sprawling onto the deck. It took him a minute to get on his feet again, and March had a sinking fear that he was badly hurt, but she dared not take her hands from the wheel. When he did stand up she could see that blood was running down the side of his face, but he ignored it and, clinging tightly to the side of the boat, began once more shouting Caitlin's name.

"Maybe I could reach her by radio," March called out, but Ted shook his head. "You'd be wasting your time. Caitlin would never think about monitoring Channel 16." She knew he was right and began to feel a sickening sureness that Caitlin and Penny had been thrown overboard in the heavy seas. She was maneuvering her boat cautiously around for another circle of the smaller boat when they saw a bedraggled Caitlin emerge unsteadily from the tiny cabin in the bow, looking pale and seasick. March's heart gave a leap.

"Caitlin! Is Penny all right?"

Caitlin managed to nod, then grabbed the side of the boat and leaned over it, unglamorously sick.

"Caitlin, listen to me!" March shouted when the girl had turned back toward her. "I don't care how sick you are. You must do exactly as I say or we'll all die out here." She could feel Ted's startled reaction and turned to see him staring at her, white-faced and

185

with blood trickling down his cheek. The first large raindrops were just starting to fall. "We'll be all right, Ted," she reassured him. "But Caitlin has to be scared into action, I'm afraid."

"Do exactly as March says, Caitlin!" Ted yelled. And to March, "What's first?"

"Tell them to put on life preservers at once," she ordered, and Ted cupped his hands and relayed it to Caitlin in his stronger voice. The rain was coming down harder. March saw Penny, white-faced and scared-looking, creep out of the cabin after Caitlin and start to put on a life jacket. It seemed to take the two of them an eternity. When at last they had finished she said to Ted, "Tell them they must anchor and ride out the storm. We'll do the same."

Ted looked aghast. "Anchor here? In all this? Can't we throw them a tow line and get away from these reefs?"

March shook her head firmly. Sheets of gray water were lashing at them now. "Impossible," she said. "We'd never make it back in this." There was no time to explain the hazards to him, but she knew them well—the danger of towing a boat in a following sea— which is what they would have on the way back. The *Flower*'s stern could be thrown about by overtaking waves, and Caitlin's boat, momentarily out of control, could come racing up behind her in a trough and. . . . March veered away from thinking about what might happen next.

"Give her these instructions, Ted," March said. "She must go back down into the cabin and open the hatch in the bow of the boat. Tell her to climb up carefully through the hatch and let out the anchor. She knows how to do it; she's done it before." Ted relayed the orders but Caitlin only stared back at them numbly.

March shouted at her. "Take a look at those reefs behind you, Caitlin. You're blowing toward them and so are we. Now move!"

186

She went on circling the boat slowly and agonizing over Caitlin's slowness, but at last the girl went into the cabin and then appeared through the hatch. For a fleeting moment March could not help feeling pity for her. It was a hard thing to do in rough water, even for someone experienced. After a struggle Caitlin managed to get the anchor off the bow and into the water, but at that moment a huge wave hit the boat and she was thrown back down into the cabin. Slowly she pulled herself back up through the hatch, and this time Penny followed her.

"Penny, be careful!" March cried, but the little girl moved ahead to help with the anchor. Her small face, which had been pale and frightened moments before, was set in a determined look.

"Let out more line!" March ordered, and Ted echoed it. "More line! More! The angle of the line is still too steep. It won't hold! That's better."

When she was satisfied that the anchor was holding she gave orders for them to secure the hatch and then go back down into the cabin and stay inside no matter what. Between them the two girls managed to batten the hatch and then disappeared below. Ted was alrcady letting out their own anchor. When it was secured, with the *Flower* rocking wildly in the downpour but holding fast, March cut the motor and said firmly, "Now we'll go below ourselves and ride it out."

"You go," Ted said. "I'll stay here and keep an eye on them."

"I'm the captain here," March countered. "We go below. You're hurt, and I want to take a look at that cut on your head. There's nothing you can accomplish by staying up here. We'll check on them every few minutes." Reluctantly he followed her below into the small cabin. In spite of the rolling of the boat, she managed to bring out the first aid kit and swab the cut on his head with disinfectant. The bleeding had largely

187

stopped. He seemed almost unaware of his own injury. His eyes were wide and distraught, his light hair plastered to his head. He seemed totally unaware of the blood that had stained his life jacket and windbreaker. For the first time March realized the truth of something she had only suspected before, that he really loved Caitlin, and she said softly, "We'll get them back safely, Ted. Don't worry. It'll be all right." *Now if I could only manage to believe that myself*, she thought desperately.

She made him sit still for the twenty minutes or so it took the downpour to let up. "You'll need your strength later," she told him. She herself went out at intervals to be sure the small boat was holding fast. At last the rain diminished and then gradually the winds began to subside as the squall moved on past them. Both she and Ted went up on deck. They could see that the blackest of the clouds had moved to the east. Skies overhead were gray and the seas still choppy, but unmistakably, the worst was over. She started the motor and gave orders to Ted to pull up the anchor, and they began to circle the small boat again.

With the passing of the storm Ted's spirits seemed to have picked up, and March did not disillusion him, even though she could see how perilously close they were to the reefs. The most dangerous part was still ahead of them. She knew she must execute the towing without any mistakes. Ted was shouting to Caitlin and Penny, and after a moment the two of them came cautiously out of the cabin. Caitlin had a large bump on her head from her fall through the hatch, but they seemed otherwise unhurt.

"Try to start your boat, Caitlin!" March called out.

Caitlin turned the key and the motor caught but then sputtered out and died. She repeated it twice with the same results, and looked helplessly toward March, both palms spread out.

"Sounds as if the fuel isn't getting through," March said. "I'll bet she didn't bother to fill the gas tank."

"She did go tearing out of there in an awful hurry."

"So the gas is low in the tank and the fuel line is probably clogged with dirt from the bottom of the tank. All right, we're going to have to tow them," March said decisively. "There's a heavy nylon line in the rear side compartment. Bring it out." The *Flower* was never without such an emergency line; the captain had insisted on it, and nylon made a good tow line, because of its springiness, which would ease heavy shocks during the tow. Ted brought it out and March said, "I'm going to approach them as close as I dare. You're going to have to toss the line to them."

Ted nodded, his jaw set grimly, and began throwing the line toward Caitlin as March circled slowly around her. After Caitlin had made several fruitless attempts to catch it, Penny joined her. The small face was set and determined, and with surprising coordination, she caught the line neatly on the second try.

"Good girl, Penny! Fasten it to that forward cleat!" March ordered, and the two girls managed it between them. "Are you sure it'll hold?" March demanded, and it was Penny who answered, "It'll hold, March!"

Ted was already fastening his end of the line to the stern of the boat, but March stopped him. "Use a cleat further forward, Ted. If you tie it to the stern the pull will prevent the stern from swinging properly in response to the rudder action; it'll interfere with the boat's maneuvering ability."

For a moment Ted looked at her with astonishment. "You do know your business, Captain!" he said admiringly, and March answered softly, as she had answered Penny the other day, "Someone taught me."

When both ends of the two lines were secure, March called out, "I'm going to inch ahead to take the tension off your anchor line. Then you'll have to pull it up." Penny seemed to understand at once and nodded. Caitlin had a confused look on her ashen

189

face. She appeared close to tears or hysteria or both, and March had a moment's sinking feeling that, having reached the crucial point, she would collapse. Ted must have had the same feeling, for suddenly he called out in the sharpest voice March had ever heard him use to Caitlin, "Don't just stand there, Caitlin; help her with that anchor. She can't do it alone!"

Caitlin seemed to give a little start and looked at Ted oddly, but she moved to grab the anchor line along with Penny and between them they eased it up out of the water as March pulled forward slowly.

"Okay!" she shouted. "We're on our way!" She glanced back over her shoulder and made a circle of her thumb and forefinger. Penny caught the gesture and returned it. "Now keep your eye on that line, Ted," she warned him. "If the pressure on its gets too great and it snaps, it'll come whipping forward like a huge rubber band. You don't want to get hurt twice."

"Aye aye, Captain," he said, but she could tell that some of the anxiety had left his voice. Now at last she snapped on the ship-to-shore radio, found Channel 16 and reported their safety and whereabouts. This time Paulie's voice had lost all pretense of calmness. March could hear her sobbing with relief.

"Oh, March, we were so worried."

"Is Tommy back yet?" She did not ask about Simon.

"Not yet. The rain probably held them up."

"See you in a few minutes. Over and out," March said.

Slowly and carefully she eased her boat to port and started back through the choppy sea toward the shelter of the marina. She breathed a quiet prayer of thanks as her hand slid over the smooth wheel, and suddenly words from her childhood came back to her. A favorite Bible story which she had teased the Captain to read to her over and over. *And he arose, and rebuked the wind, and said unto the sea, Peace, be still . . .*

190

She had hoped to avoid Simon when she reached the marina. She had had all the emotion she could handle for one day, but she was doomed to disappointment. By the time the *Flower of the Sea* pulled in with the smaller boat in tow, she could see both Tommy and Simon at the dock, furiously tearing the sodden tarpaulin off Tommy's boat and casting off the lines. They stopped when they saw March's boat enter the quiet water with Caitlin's following, and rushed to help the two boats in to the dock. March took one look at Simon's white face, drawn into lines of fear and then subsiding into relief as he caught sight of Penny cheerfully waving to him and shouting, "Hi, Daddy!" At once March looked away, busying herself with nosing the *Flower* into its berth. Ted tossed the nylon line to Tommy, who used it to pull the powerless boat in.

"Well done, Captain," Ted said quietly, and March glancing at him, thought that he wore a different look from the Ted who had started out with her.

"I had a good first mate," she answered, trying to smile at him but feeling suddenly so exhausted that she could hardly stand. *Very nicely done, Captain.* That was what Simon had said to her that day they had navigated the reefs on their way to Whispering Pines.

"Come on, leave all that," Ted said, seeing her reach for the canvas cover. "I'll come back later and make everything shipshape for you. Right now you need dry clothes, and I think something hot might be in order."

"I'm all right, Ted, really," she answered weakly, but she did not argue. She pulled herself out of the boat and up onto the dock just as a tearful Paulie came running toward her.

"March! Oh, thank heavens!" she exploded, catching March in her arms and hugging her tight. "What a thing to do to all of us! When that storm hit I thought we'd never see you again."

191

March hugged her back with what strength she could muster.

"Come on in this minute," Paulie ordered. "Your teeth are chattering and you're soaked through. You've got to get into some dry clothes."

March allowed herself a quick glance in Simon's direction. He and Tommy had pulled the small boat up parallel with the dock and were helping Caitlin and Penny out of it. She saw him clasp the little girl in his arms as she climbed out. His back was to March, his head bent forward over Penny's shoulder in an attitude that looked almost prayerful. *How I would like to think it really is that*, March thought, and swallowed a painful lump that had risen in her own throat.

"You're right, Paulie. I believe I could do with a little warming up," she said hurriedly. "Let's get inside, shall we?" Out of the corner of her eye she thought she saw him straighten up and turn toward her just as she and Paulie walked away, but she did not wait.

For the next hour March allowed herself to give in shamelessly to the unfamiliar sensation of being waited on, petted, praised, and indulged. She soaked in a hot tub in Paulie's bathroom, then let herself be bundled into slacks and a fluffy blue sweater of Paulie's—everything a bit large for her but warm and cosily comforting. Marian Sanders came hurrying with a mug of piping hot chocolate, which she insisted March drink down to the very bottom while she stood over her, watching and shaking her head in a kind of proud despair. Paulie toweled her hair, then used the blow dryer on it, brushing it out and saying—it seemed to March with every other stroke of the brush – "And *then* what happened?"

By the time she had gone over the details of the afternoon repeatedly, March felt warmed through, pleasantly relaxed, and sleepy from the comforting drink. She had not been so fussed over since the afternoon she had spent in Rene's in New York with Melissa. *How long ago?* she thought sleepily. Scarcely more than a week. Was it possible?

Paulie, still keyed up, maintained a barrage of questions and exclamations. "That Caitlin Massie could have gotten you all killed!" "Honestly, someone should take after that girl with a hairbrush; I mean, she really deserves a good whack." "Of all the irresponsible . . . " "What could Simon Wade have been thinking of to let her look after his daughter?"

March, trying to stem her friend's indignation, answered, "I'm sure after the snorkeling incident he thought she'd learned her lesson."

"People like Caitlin never learn their lessons," Paulie retorted. March did not answer, partly because she could not trust herself to discuss Simon in a rational way, and partly because she was not entirely sure Paulie was wrong, at least where Caitlin was concerned. March found that the room around her was growing blurry and her eyelids were beginning to prickle. Paulie turned the dryer off and said, "Oh March, here I am rattling on as usual and you're exhausted. Come on now. Lie down here and I'll cover you. Take a good nap while I go downstairs for a while. The Florida plane's late today on account of the storm, but it'll be along soon, and we have guests arriving. I'll have to help in the lobby. I'll come back after you've had a chance to rest."

March nodded wearily and sank back on the pillow as Paulie raised her feet up onto the bed and covered her with a light blanket. March did not even hear the door close as she went out. Marcus, the cat settled down close to her shoulder and began to purr softly.

She sank almost at once into a deep soft sleep in which she seemed to be dropping down further and further into darkness, but it was not an unpleasant darkness. Rather it was a warm and reassuring one, with softness and comfort all around her, pressing in from every side. A nice place to stay, her mind kept telling her. Perhaps she would simply stay on forever and never climb back up to the surface. Then suddenly the sensations seemed to change slightly, so that instead of warmth and softness, the protective cocoon-like layer around her dropped away and she was left alone in the dark. When she reached out with her arms she could feel nothing around her. She was in a void, completely isolated, and the darkness was no longer comforting and pleasant, but menacing, as if it held danger within it.

She let out a little cry of fear and then suddenly someone was holding her in strong arms that protected and comforted. She was sitting up in bed, her head on his chest. She could feel his cheek resting against her hair.

"You're all right," he whispered. "You were dreaming. You're all right now."

She was not fully awake and it seemed an odd and puzzling thing that he should be here with her. But there was no mistaking the strength of the hard-muscled body, the fresh outdoor scent, the deep voice offering comfort.

He said softly, "I've been waiting forever to come to you. They said you were resting and I wasn't to disturb you."

She opened her eyes drowsily. She must have slept a long time, she thought, for the room had a purple, shadowed look. She closed them again and gave in to the bliss of being enfolded in his arms. "I was so afraid," she murmured. "I was all alone." Suddenly memory came flooding back. "Is Penny all right?" she asked, pulling back a little and looking up at him. In the dim twilight she could see the look of tenderness on his face.

"Sound asleep too. She's fine. March, little March, how can I ever thank you for what you did?"

March looked down again, shaking her head against his chest, but his arms held her close. "It wasn't anything," she said, thinking how foolish it sounded. She wanted so much to say the right thing, to strike just the right note of distance and formality. She did not want to care again, but it was hopeless. There was no way she could keep herself from responding to the heat of his body, the answering warmth of her own. There was no way she could tell her heart to stop its pounding, or her nerves to cease their restless tingling urges.

"It was absolutely incredible, what you did. I still can't believe it. When Tommy and I got back and Paulie told us—not that we got a very straight story from her. She was pretty close to hysteria by then. That's when we tore out on the dock, to take after you in his boat. I was frantic. We'd seen the storm and how bad it was as we drove back from Johnsville. The causeway road was under a foot of water. And then when I realized you and Penny were out in it. . . . " All his fears and anxieties seemed to come pouring out, and March was content to let him talk as long as she could rest there in his arms, feeling the strength of his body sustaining her. It was Penny, of course, whom he had been worried about; that was to be expected, and his gratitude was in proportion to that worry. *Still, he had said you and Penny. What do I care?* March thought blissfully. *What do I care about his reason for saying it?*

He pressed her head against his chest, kissing her hair and saying, "How can I ever tell you how grateful I am?"

Feeling the closeness and warmth between them, March wondered whether she might say the thing that was in her heart—the thing that had been hiding in the back of her awareness ever since she had seen him embrace Penny on the dock.

She said a little hesitantly, "Has it occurred to you,

Simon, that perhaps some other hand than mine helped bring Penny back safely? That someone might have given me the strength I needed and that I was only working through Him?''

She looked up into his face and saw him frown, thinking about it. "I'm not sure what you mean.''

"I mean that perhaps Penny was saved for a reason. To help bring you to Christ.'' She had said it as simply as she knew how. And he gave her a direct look.

"Do you believe that could happen?''

"With all my heart.'' A joyful singing sounded inside her head.

Slowly he released her and stood up. March got up, too, and stood on the other side of the bed. The cat, still snoozing, opened a wary eye and glanced from one to the other. March went on looking at Simon in the dim twilight of the room, not speaking for fear of disrupting whatever was working inside him. For long moments he stood there, his hands in his pockets, his eyes lowered. He seemed to be thinking about what she had said, concentrating hard. Then he lifted his head and she saw an alteration in his features. Once again they had hardened into the old worldly look she had come to know so well.

"Well, who knows?'' he shrugged, and started for the door. March's heart turned cold with disappointment as she turned and walked to the window, from where, far off along the airport road, she could see Ed Beaslie's sturdy taxi plodding toward the inn. She clasped her arms in front of her as though holding tight to herself for courage. "Just keep an eye on Penny in the future, won't you? And keep her away from Caitlin?''

"Yes. I'm afraid I deserved that,'' he said. She could hear the irony in his voice, could even picture his mouth twisting in that quirk she had seen before. The old distance was back between them now. He sounded cold and withdrawn. All the warmth, the passion, the closeness had vanished. They were two strangers. Adversaries even. And a world divided them.

"Goodbye, March." She heard him leave the room, and the click of the door's closing seemed to punctuate his last words. Only then did March turn away from the window, and her hand came up to cover her mouth as sudden tears coursed down her cheeks there in the empty room. For a long time she stood in a kind of stupor, numb and unfeeling, every part of her body echoing the finality of his leaving. Then the unmistakable rattle of the island's taxi sounded below her at the entance to the inn, and she turned slowly to look down at it. Stout Ed Beaslie climbed out of the van and began to hand down luggage, leaving his passengers to fend for themselves as he always did. Doors opened and the new arrivals began to step out. March reached up to brush away her tears and started to turn from the window when something caught her attention. She gave a start and looked back. From Paulie's room which was at an angle to the main entrance, she could see quite clearly, and now she stared incredulously at one of the passengers who had just stepped out and now stood looking around her in the soft sunset dusk that had followed the storm. It was, unmistakably, the beautiful Diana of the plane trip, the one who had accompanied Simon from New York and who had clung to him so wistfully as he tried to bundle her into a taxi at the airport. She was a picture of sophistication and style in her exquisitely tailored linen suit, and her look was the same aloof one, faintly touched with boredom, that March had noticed on the plane. A man had gotten out after her, and they appeared to be together, for he said something to her in a low voice and she responded. March could hear their voices but could not make out the words. The woman's voice was unmistakable, however—slow, elegant, well modulated.

While she watched, March saw someone else—Simon Wade—appear below her. He had come out onto the veranda and now paused for a moment on the top step. She could almost read his surprise in the way he stood there staring at the taxi and the new arrivals. Then he called out, and she could hear it quite clearly, "Diana! What are *you* doing here? Ed—I didn't expect you until tomorrow!" And without hesitation he hurried down the steps and enfolded the woman in his arms. Even from this distance March could see that there was a warmth in their greeting. It was more than just casual. There was something comfortable and warm about it. *It has reality*, she thought. *With me it was all make-believe, but this is real. You can tell the difference. They're two people who are alike, who come from the same world, and whatever is between them shows. You can read it plainly. Even Caitlin Massie with all her father's money doesn't belong in that world.*

She watched as the woman took his arm again and clung to it as they walked up the steps and into the inn. "I made him bring me, that's all," the woman's voice drifted up to where March was standing at the now opened window. They disappeared from her view, and for a long time March did not move, but simply stood there lost in thought and watching the last moments of the sun setting in a rosy-purple glory over the sea, which had turned quietly peaceful after the storm.

"How about some dinner?" Paulie's voice made her start, and she turned to see her friend standing at her elbow and looking out at the sunset along with her.

"Paulie, I didn't hear you come in. Oh, I'm not very hungry. And besides, I'm not really dressed for the dining room."

"March, you're such a celebrity today you could show up in a potato sack and still get a standing ovation. Everyone's talking about what you did. And I never saw anyone so grateful as Simon Wade. He couldn't believe it."

"Yes. He came up here and thanked me," March said carefully.

Paulie was scanning her face anxiously, but the room was in deep shadow now. "He really seemed— oh, you know—he did seem to mean it, March."

"I'm sure he did. His daughter means everything to him." Even to her own ears her voice had a brittle sound."

There was a silence of hesitation between them, but Paulie was not one to ask unwelcome questions. Instead she said, "How about if I bring something up here for both of us on a tray?"

"Don't bother, Paulie. You must be terribly busy down at the desk, getting everyone registered."

"I was, but Daddy came in and he's finishing it."

"Two of the people seem to have come to meet Simon."

"Yes. The man's named Edward Fenton. We had a reservation for him, only for tomorrow. We managed to squeeze him in. Gave him that small room in back. I think he's with Simon Wade's company. The woman—her name's Diana something. Barrington, I think."

"They seem to be old friends."

"Yes. We had a hard time finding a place for her. We're pretty full."

"Oh?"

"Yes. Then she said she wouldn't mind sharing with the little girl – with Penny."

In the room adjoining Simon's, March thought.

CHAPTER 12

THE *AYES OF TEXAS* pulled majestically out of the marina next morning, bound for home, but not before Stan Massie had showered March with effusive thanks and extracted from her a promise to come and visit them in Texas or Palm Beach, wherever she chose.

"If it was anybody else I'd offer 'em a reward for the kind of thing you did, honey," he said, still shaking his head in wonderment as he had been doing ever since he had heard, on his return the night before, all the details of the rescue. "But I know better'n to do that with you. Best I can do is offer you our Texas hospitality any time you care to sample it. And if you ever need anything—now I mean anything at *all* —you just don't be afraid to let me know, you hear?"

"I hear, Stan," March smiled. "And I'll remember it, too."

"And I'll take care of shipping your fish to Florida for mounting," Tommy assured him, helping with the lines and fenders.

"Goodbye, March," Ted said, kissing her lightly. "I wouldn't have missed it. Can't say any more than that."

"Goodbye, Ted. I hope everything turns out right for you." She was not sure she should wish him to win Caitlin Massie. But she had a new respect for him after yesterday and she really did hope that life gave him what he wanted.

Caitlin was subdued, less arrogant than formerly as she hung back and said her goodbyes from a slight distance.

"Thank you for all you did, March," she said, and the words seemed to come awkwardly, as though it were not a thing she was accustomed to.

March smiled at her and noticed that Caitlin's hand slid into Ted's as they stood there on the dock.

"Goodbye, Caitlin. I hope we meet again sometime." *But not too soon*, March thought with some inward reservation. *I'll need a little time to recover.*

She had come to the dock to work on her own boat, to give it a final scrubbing and polishing before turning it over to the Hollisters, and now she collected her bucket and brushes and stood watching as the big yacht moved gracefully out toward open water. Stan Massie looked back over his shoulder to wave from his position at the wheel and Monica, trailing gold chains and silk scarves, leaned over the railing as she waved. "Bye bye, Marge!" Her voice drifted back, growing fainter.

March gave a last wave, turned and started toward shore. Now that the boat was cleaned she would finish up whatever remained to be done at the house, and tomorrow she would meet the Hollisters in Johnsville at the lawyer's office. This would be her last night in the house as its owner. And even though the Hollisters had told her she must take her time and not rush to vacate the place, March had no wish to linger once the sale was concluded. She had already telephoned

201

the airline for her reservation. Day after tomorrow she would be gone from Coral Cay. Melissa, in New York, had been ecstatic at hearing it. "Wonderful, March! Now give me the flight number so we can meet you." March, at her end, had tried to project enthusiasm over the miles between them, but must have failed, for Melissa added with concern, "Are you all right? Everything okay?"

"Everything's fine, Melissa," March had answered firmly. "See you soon."

Back at the house she went on with her packing. Books, records, her shell collection, her own clothing. She was once again in her old jeans and denim shirt, and her red bandana. As she stacked and packed and sorted she also scrubbed and dusted shelves and furniture. She wanted to leave the house looking its best, just as she had with the boat. The Hollisters were happy with its present furniture, so she was leaving it for them, and although there was a heaviness around her heart, she did find some comfort in the work itself. *I must stop feeling sorry for myself*, she scolded inwardly. 8it I'll have money enough to settle my bills and maybe a little bit over if I'm lucky. I have Melissa and Bill to help me get settled. I even have a job waiting. And the house and boat will be going to people I like who'll take good care of them.

The knock at the door made her pause, dustcloth in hand, and for a moment she stood quite still in the midst of the clutter and wondered if she could simply not answer it. There was no one she wanted to see at this moment, even Paulie. She needed to be alone to arrange her thoughts, to scold herself into an acceptance of what was coming. Least of all did she want to see Simon again before she left. Still, that was not a likelihood, since he would be busy entertaining the beautiful Diana Barrington. It might possibly be Penny, if Paulie had happened to tell her March would be leaving soon. Penny might be coming to say goodbye. *And Penny is the one person I guess I wouldn't mind seeing*, March thought, and went to open the door.

But it was Simon standing there, his face serious, without a trace of a smile, the muscle in his cheek moving tautly.

"Good morning," March said, but there was no welcome in her voice even though her heart had turned over at the sight of him.

His dark eyes studied her with a peculiar intensity and for a moment he said nothing. Then in a low voice he said, "I've just heard that you will be leaving Coral Cay soon."

"Yes, day after tomorrow."

"It's final? It's settled?"

"Yes. I've sold my house to Mr. and Mrs. Hollister. They've vacationed here on Coral Cay for many years. We're to close the deal at the lawyer's office tomorrow. And my boat—they'll be taking that too. I've already made my plane reservation."

"I'm sorry to hear it," he said, still in the low voice. "I had hoped – that is, it seemed to me . . . " The words trailed off and then he said, "I wonder if I could come in for a minute."

"Oh, of course," she said, and stood aside to let him in. He stood there in his knit shirt and slacks, dressed as she had become used to seeing him, and she moved away so that several feet of floor space separated them. He glanced around at the cartons she was packing. "Well. This does look like business."

She said, with an attempt at polite remoteness, "How is your building project coming? Have you received your government approval yet?"

"I have been assured it will be granted this week."

"That's really unusual speed. Congratulations. Then you'll be starting work at once?"

"Yes, as soon as the men and heavy equipment arrive."

"Excavation? Road-building?" In spite of her best efforts, she could not manage to keep the bitterness out of her voice.

"A few preliminary things," he shrugged.

Without meaning to, March glanced toward the captain's map of Whispering Pines Cay, which she had left out on the table. He saw the look and followed it.

"I know you dislike me for my work," he said, and then he added sardonically, "among other things."

"Please. There's no need to discuss any of this any more. Let's part friends and let it go at that. I won't be here to criticize what you do." Quickly, before he could speak again, she asked. "How's Penny today? No after-effects?"

"None at all, apparently. The resiliency of the young."

"I meant to tell you how very well she behaved through it all. How quickly she followed every instruction and didn't panic. She's a remarkable little girl."

"She thinks a great deal of you."

"I thought she might be coming here for a last visit."

"She will, of course. I asked her to stay with Diana for now."

March could not help feeling a touch of curiosity over how the svelte Diana Barrington was managing a lively seven-year-old.

"I saw her on the plane with you coming from New York," March said.

"Diana? Ah yes. I'd forgotten."

"She's very beautiful."

"Yes, she is that."

"And Penny is fond of her?"

"They seem to get on well together."

"Yet she seems so well-groomed—so elegant. I wouldn't think . . . "

"You mean you can't imagine her coping with a lively young child?" He gave her a curious look as though something was just now occurring to him.

"Well, I only mean . . ."

"I think I know what you meant," he said slowly. "But actually you're quite mistaken. In fact right now I think you'd find Diana pretty much pulled apart and Penny giving her a new hairdo. Although when I left them just now both of them were on the floor doing a jigsaw puzzle of astounding complexity."

"I hadn't pictured her like that," March said softly. Somehow it was painful to her, his affectionate description of this other woman.

"Oh, she was always like that. If you knew her at all you'd soon become aware of her other side."

Not likely, March thought, with a painful inward twist.

"The fact is, my sister's trouble has always been with men. She lets them take advantage of her, and then I'm left to pick up the pieces and stand by patiently till the broken heart mends, which seldom takes long, thank goodness."

"Your sister?" Realization of what he was saying hit March suddenly. His eyes, which had been dark and serious, held a light that looked suspiciously like a twinkle of amusement.

"Yes, but I think she's beginning to realize that what she needs is a good steady dependable fellow like Ed Fenton. I've been praising him to her for years. He's always loved her."

"Your sister," March whispered. Then she collected herself and said as calmly as she could over the pounding of her heart, "Well, thank you for coming to say goodbye."

"I didn't come here to say goodbye."

"You didn't?" March's eyebrows went up.

"No. I came to show you something."

March did not answer. What could he possibly want to show her that she would be interested in seeing?

"My plans for Whispering Pines Cay."

March felt her whole body stiffen with resentment as she noticed for the first time that he was carrying the familiar rolled-up drawing paper under his arm.

"Really, I'd rather not," she said.

"It will only take a moment," he said. "Surely you can spare me that." And then, in a softer voice, "I wanted to show them to you after that first day you took me there in your boat. Except that you came on so strong about my work—how much you disliked everything about it—well, perhaps I was too proud after that."

"I didn't mean to do that. But it's a place that's always meant a great deal to me, and to my father."

"I know, and I was the intruder," he said wryly. "You certainly made that clear enough. I'd bought it sight unseen, through an agent. I saw it for the first time that day with you. But I loved it right away. Somehow I'd known I would. The descriptions I'd had of it made me feel it wasn't going to be just an investment. I'd felt right along it was going to be a place I would grow very close to, and as soon as I saw it I knew I was right. Knowing you felt the same way about it was one of the things that made me love you."

Warmth flared into March's cheeks and her breath caught in a little gasp.

"Yes. I have to say it now even though you dislike me so much. It was why I was furious that night of the party. I was so sure you were different. I didn't want to believe you were deliberately trying to hurt me with that business of Gina's record, but I didn't see what else it could be."

"But I didn't know," March breathed.

"I realized that later, but by then I'd stupidly made everything worse. And I never could seem to get back on that footing with you that we'd had the afternoon we walked to the little church and then went out to the reef diving."

"That was such a wonderful day," March said, almost without meaning to.

"I saw the real you that day for the first time, I think. I guess it was something about that old church and the conch shell to call the kids. I saw you as you must have been in those days. I could see you as a little girl going to that church. I even loved that little girl—that little March Raffin that you were then. And later when you lectured me for being a bad father I suppose I got sore because I knew you were so right. I thought, if only I'd been able to give my daughter what you had, I could even see Penny going to that Sunday school . . ." He hesitated, then said simply, "I want her to have your faith, March."

She asked softly, "And you? Don't you need faith too?"

He made a gesture of dismissal with one hand. "It's too late for me. Anyway, it doesn't matter."

"It does matter," March insisted. "And it's never too late to come to Jesus Christ, to accept him in your life."

He stared at her in wonderment. "You say that so easily. Almost as if you were talking about a friend."

"I am," March said. "And he would be your friend, too, if you would let him." She stayed quiet then, hardly daring to breathe. Something precious and fragile seemed to hang suspended between them. She scarcely dared move for fear of breaking it. But then suddenly he moved away from her and the moment seemed to have vanished as he turned businesslike once more. He crossed to the table where the captain's map lay.

"I saw this— just a glimpse of it—that first time I came to your house," he said. "And I was astounded, because even the quick glance I had showed me that it was a map of Whispering Pines. And more than that, that some ideas for construction had been roughly sketched in."

"It was my father's sketch," March said. "But it was just daydreaming. His idea of what could be done with the island—what he'd have done if it had been his."

Yes, that's what I thought it must be." He paused. "I wish I could have known him," he said as if to himself. Then he went on more briskly, unrolling the sketch he had been carrying, "Because what astounded me . . . " He laid the drawing out alongside the captain's, weighing the corners down with books. "It was exactly how I was planning to develop the island. I'd made this drawing in my room at the inn that night after we'd returned from the island. Look, here's where I thought a small inn might be situated. And the marina here, of course, where the good landing is. And dotted through here . . . " His hand moved over the drawing, long brown finger pointing as he spoke. March moved quietly over to stand beside him and look at it. "That's were the small cottages would be— but well hidden from one another to preserve the beauty of the island, and for privacy too, because remember I told you this island would be for a certain kind of vacationer. Not necessarily the wealthy, but those looking for a special kind of place and a special kind of privacy. People with an appreciation for the island's beauty—and a respect for it."

"And that was what you were planning all along?" March whispered. "No high rises, no shops, no casinos?"

"No, never. Only you didn't give me a chance to explain what my plans really were."

"No," she admitted quietly. "I never did, did I?"

He left the table and walked to the window, standing there with his back to her, looking out. In a quiet voice he said, "I've thought a great deal about what you said to me, that perhaps Penny's life was spared for a purpose. To bring me—well, you said to bring me to Christ. Do you really think that might be true?"

"I have already told you so," March said simply. "I believe it with all my heart."

"But you have so much inner strength," he said. "I wonder if I could ever attain that."

"Oh Simon, if you knew how often I fall short. . ."

"You? I can't believe it."

"Yes, it's true, but I always know I'm forgiven, just as I try to forgive. And Simon, that's the one thing. . . ." She paused, for this part was difficult. "You must learn to forgive Gina, truly you must. I know how hard your heart is toward her, but you can never really accept Christ with that rancor inside. Forgiving her would be the first step in a whole new life for you."

For a moment he did not answer her, and then it seemed to her something in his face changed, grew softer, as if all the old sardonic lines had erased themselves. "Do you know, March?" he said in a wondering voice, "I think I have already forgiven her? I think because of what almost happened to Penny I kept thinking in the midst of all my fear how Penny was Gina's child as well, and somehow I couldn't hate her any more,"

"Didn't I tell you?" March whispered. "Didn't I tell you there was a purpose behind it all?"

She crossed the room to stand close to him. He reached out for her hands. "Will you help me, March?"

"You know I will. Every step of the way."

"And Penny?"

"Of course, Penny already longs for the reassurance of faith; I can feel it in her."

The moment lay between them, too thick with meaning to admit more words, until at last Simon sighed. But not the old world-weary sigh that March had heard before; rather a sigh of fulfillment. *A corner has been turned*, March thought.

"Now there's another problem facing me."

"I think you can face anything now."

"Perhaps. That's for you to tell me. Now that I've learned how much these islands mean to you, how much you love Whispering Pines, I'm afraid to ask you. . . ."

"Ask me what?"

"To marry me," he said, and let his breath out in a rush.

"Oh, Simon. Marriage? So soon? You hardly know me!" But the joyous singing went on inside her.

"I know all I need to know," he said, smiling down at her with that odd little one-sided smile that was tender and yet held a hint of sadness. "I know you're totally enchanting, and beautiful, although I suspect you don't quite realize how beautiful. I know you're brave and resourceful. You have a rare kind of loyalty, and beyond all that. . . ." His eyes searched her face. "You have a faith that I want to learn to share. You did mean it when you said it wasn't too late for me?"

"Of course it's not too late," she said warmly. "And oh, Simon, the joy it will bring to your life!" She felt her heart turning over almost painfully, and warmth flooded into her cheeks. Love, which had been there all along, but which she had tried so hard to avoid recognizing, seemed to fill her whole being. "But you used a word just now, share. You said you wanted to learn to share with me—thoughts, beliefs, feelings—so many things, I suppose you meant. I loved it when you said that. But Simon, all that takes time. There's so much we must learn about each other. And there's Penny. I don't want to jump right into the middle of your two lives without knowing her better, too. It wouldn't be fair. Let's take these next few months while you're working at Whispering Pines to become better friends."

He was looking down at her tenderly. "You aren't angry with me any more—about Whispering Pines?"

"How could I be, now that I know your plans for it? Besides, the island will always be there for us, won't it, whenever we want to come to it."

"Yes, of course."

"Then I won't really have lost it, will I?" She hesitated, then said, smiling a little, "I don't think I'm going to need a hideaway island of my own any more. I think my life is going to be quite full without it."

He pulled her to him and she pressed her cheek against his chest, feeling the ripple of muscles under his shirt. "I'm not much of a catch any more," she said in a teasing voice. "I've gotten rid of everything—my house, my boat. . . ."

"You'll be bringing me something much more valuable," he whispered. "Anyway, I'll have my own flower of the sea, won't I!"

ABOUT THE AUTHOR

AMANDA CLARK is the pseudonym for a prolific mother/daughter writing team. They have produced several books as a team, as well as publishing novels, magazine articles, and even teachers' guides individually. Along with book and magazine writing, both have worked as newspaper reporters and editors. FLOWER OF THE SEA is their first Serenade Serenata title, a testimony to their faith in God's guidance in every area of our lives.

A Letter To Our Readers

Dear Reader:

In order that we might better contribute to your reading enjoyment, we would appreciate your taking a few minutes to respond to the following questions and return to:

Editor, Serenade Books
The Zondervan Publishing House
1415 Lake Drive, S.E.
Grand Rapids, Michigan 49506

1. Did you enjoy reading FLOWER OF THE SEA?

   ☐ Very much. I would like to see more books by this author!
   ☐ Moderately
   ☐ I would have enjoyed it more if _____

2. Where did you purchase this book? _____

3. What influenced your decision to purchase this book?

   ☐ Cover   ☐ Back cover copy
   ☐ Title   ☐ Friends
   ☐ Publicity   ☐ Other _____

4. Would you be interested in reading other Serenade/ Serenata or Serenade/Saga Books?

☐ Very interested
☐ Moderately interested
☐ Not interested

5. Please indicate your age range:

☐ Under 18   ☐ 25–34   ☐ 46–55
☐ 18–24   ☐ 35–45   ☐ Over 55

6. Would you be interested in a Serenade book club? If so, please give us your name and address:

Name _____

Occupation _____

Address _____

City _____ State _____ Zip _____

Serenade Saga books are inspirational romances in historical settings, designed to bring you a joyful, heart-lifting reading experience.

Serenade Saga books available in your local book store:

#1 SUMMER SNOW, Sandy Dengler
#2 CALL HER BLESSED, Jeanette Gilge
#3 INA, Karen Baker Kletzing
#4 JULIANA OF CLOVER HILL,
    Brenda Knight Graham
#5 SONG OF THE NEREIDS, Sandy Dengler
#6 ANNA'S ROCKING CHAIR,
    Elaine Watson
#7 IN LOVE'S OWN TIME,
    Susan C. Feldhake
#8 YANKEE BRIDE, Jane Peart
#9 LIGHT OF MY HEART, Kathleen Karr
#10 LOVE BEYOND SURRENDER,
    Susan C. Feldhake
#11 ALL THE DAYS AFTER SUNDAY,
    Jeannette Gilge
#12 WINTERSPRING, Sandy Dengler
#13 HAND ME DOWN THE DAWN,
    Mary Harwell Sayler
#14 REBEL BRIDE, Jane Peart
#15 SPEAK SOFTLY, LOVE, Kathleen Yapp
#16 FROM THIS DAY FORWARD, Kathleen Karr
#17 THE RIVER BETWEEN, Jacquelyn Cook
#18 VALIANT BRIDE, Jane Peart
#19 WAIT FOR THE SUN, Maryn Langer
#20 KINCAID OF CRIPPLE CREEK, Peggy Darty
#21 LOVE'S GENTLE JOURNEY, Kay Cornelius
#22 APPLEGATE LANDING, Jean Conrad

Serenade Serenata books are inspirational romances in contemporary settings, designed to bring you a joyful, heart-lifting reading experience.

Serenade Serenata books available in your local bookstore:

#1 ON WINGS OF LOVE, Elaine L. Schulte
#2 LOVE'S SWEET PROMISE,
    Susan C. Feldhake
#3 FOR LOVE ALONE, Susan C. Feldhake
#4 LOVE'S LATE SPRING, Lydia Heermann
#5 IN COMES LOVE, Mab Graff Hoover
#6 FOUNTAIN OF LOVE, Velma S. Daniels and
    Peggy E. King.
#7 MORNING SONG, Linda Herring
#8 A MOUNTAIN TO STAND STRONG,
    Peggy Darty
#9 LOVE'S PERFECT IMAGE, Judy Baer
#10 SMOKY MOUNTAIN SUNRISE,
    Yvonne Lehman
#11 GREENGOLD AUTUMN,
    Donna Fletcher Crow
#12 IRRESISTIBLE LOVE, Elaine Anne McAvoy
#13 ETERNAL FLAME, Lurlene McDaniel
#14 WINDSONG, Linda Herring
#15 FOREVER EDEN, Barbara Bennett
#16 CALL OF THE DOVE, Madge Harrah
#17 THE DESIRES OF YOUR HEART,
    Donna Fletcher Crow
#18 TENDER ADVERSARY, Judy Baer
#19 HALFWAY TO HEAVEN, Nancy Johanson
#20 HOLD FAST THE DREAM,
    Lurlene McDaniel
#21 THE DISGUISE OF LOVE,
    Mary LaPietra
#22 THROUGH A GLASS DARKLY,
    Sara Mitchell